SADDLE TRAMP

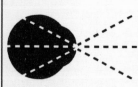

This Large Print Book carries the
Seal of Approval of N.A.V.H.

SADDLE TRAMP

A WESTERN NOVEL

TODHUNTER BALLARD

THORNDIKE PRESS
A part of Gale, Cengage Learning

Detroit • New York • San Francisco • New Haven, Conn • Waterville, Maine • London

GALE
CENGAGE Learning·

LIBRARY OF CONGRESS CATALOGING-IN-PUBLICATION DATA

Ballard, Todhunter, 1903-1980.
    Saddle tramp : a western novel / by Todhunter Ballard. — Large print ed.
      p. cm. — (Thorndike Press large print Western)
    "A shorter version of this novel appeared in The Toronto Star
Weekly"—T.p. verso.
    ISBN-13: 978-1-4104-5381-5 (hardcover)
    ISBN-10: 1-4104-5381-2 (hardcover)
    1. Large type books. I. Title.
PS3503.A5575S23 2012
813'.52—dc23   2012032596

Published in 2012 by arrangement with Golden West Literary Agency.

SADDLE TRAMP

1

Shamus Magee was happy. There had been few days during his twenty-three years when he had not been happy. He was a big man and when people made fun of his good nature he grinned.

"I'm too big to be nasty," he told them. "If I went around hunting up trouble people would call me a bully. And if I refused to fight they'd call me a coward. Way it is, I like everyone, so I never have cause to battle."

He looked around at the world in which he lived and found it good. To the west, blurred by distance, rose the central divide, its higher peaks still glistening with snow although it was the middle of July. To the east the Montrose Range, lower, but still high enough to seem to touch the arched sky.

Shamus' good feeling overflowed and he opened his mouth, singing joyfully in an off-key baritone:

The lonesomest cowboy
That ever was known
Ate garlic for breakfast
And rode all alone

Without friend or partner
Or sweetheart so dear
And even his horse made him
Mount from the rear . . .

"Stop that catawalling. Do you want to scare the horses?"

Magee turned to look at the man riding beside him. Mushy Calder was older than Magee by a dozen years, and smaller by fifty pounds and seven inches. He had a dark lean face which at times resembled a wolf's, and a temper which was as hair-triggered as Shamus' was placid. No partners in the territory were so utterly dissimilar.

"Why shucks," Magee said, not at all offended. "That there is right fancy singing if you ask me."

"I didn't ask you." Calder was nursing a more than ordinary grouch that morning. "I'm telling you to shut up before you spook the horses."

The horses were a band of two dozen

animals which they had captured on the slopes of Mont Cook, wild horses they had held in a brush corral while Magee broke them out. Now the animals were hobbled and roped together, led by a ten-year-old mare they had brought along for the purpose. Nothing short of dynamite could have forced the mare out of a walk, and she did not hesitate to use her teeth on any animal who crowded her.

The horse hunt had been Calder's idea. He was, by profession, a wolfer, hired by various ranchers to wipe out the big grey timber beasts that preyed upon the herds. He had spotted the horses early in the spring while they were still in the small valley where they had wintered, but the snow had then been too deep and he had gone for help.

He would never have found the horses but for his inordinate curiosity, which made it imperative for him to see and know everything going on in the range around him. Curiosity was the driving force of his sour life.

That he chose Magee for a partner occasioned no surprise. There was not a better man with horses in the whole country. The surprising thing was that Magee had agreed to go. Calder had few friends and many enemies. He was bad tempered and sharp tongued, and had the reputation of being a trouble-maker. Some folks even said that he was not above eating another man's beef, sharing his stolen meat with the outlaws who headquartered at the old mining camp of Hawthorn.

Magee felt this latter charge was unfair, but the fact that the wolfer roamed all over the range brought him under suspicion, and people said the only reason Calder still lived was that average sized men hesitated to kill a runt.

Sam Goth at the Belmont Bar had questioned Magee when the news leaked out that he was teaming up with Calder. "You're crazy," he told the big man. "You know what they say about him?"

"Never believed it," Magee said placidly.

"And you'll be gone maybe six weeks with no one to talk to but that human rattlesnake. You'll get so sick of his crabbing you'll break him with your hands."

"Not me," said Magee. "Trouble is, people don't understand Mushy, that's all."

"What's to understand? He's crooked and his mind is warped, and his tongue is twisted, bitter as sage."

"That's what I mean. You just don't understand him. You never took the trouble to stop and figure out why Mushy hates everyone. Well, I did. I've got the answer. It's his stomach, see. He's been eating his own cooking for the last dozen years, and believe me, Mushy is the worst cook this world ever saw." Shamus grinned and winked. "Now on this trip, I plan to do the cooking, and once that good food unsnarls his stomach he'll be all sweetness and light. You watch, just as cheerful and gay as an unspanked baby."

But the plan had not worked. Calder had grown more nasty by the day. He had smiled exactly once — on the day they caught the grey. Shamus could well understand the smile. The grey was quite a horse, the stallion that had ruled the herd. They never would have caught him if they had not managed to work him into a box canyon with walls too steep for even him to climb.

They got their ropes on him and dragged him out, biting, squealing, lashing at them with his unshod hoofs. Magee loved the grey on sight and he had taken a lot of trouble with the horse. The others he had merely busted out, but he tried to gentle the grey, tried to make friends with it. He might as well have saved his time, but he had ridden the animal, and proved to the horse that he was boss.

Calder gloated the night after they caught him. "He's worth the whole trip. The rest are scrubs, but that stallion will fetch two hundred dollars or I'm a Chinaman."

Magee thought fleetingly that the words were an insult to the Chinese or any other race Mushy might include himself in. He rather liked Wong See who ran a restaurant in Belmont, and who was the only Chinaman he knew, and by this time he had acquired a deep and abiding distaste for his partner.

Also, the idea of having to sell the grey saddened him. He wanted to keep the horse for himself, but Calder was right. The others were scrubs and if they hoped to make wages for their work they would have to be sold. The only fair way, of course, would be for Magee to try to bid him in at the sale. But he would not do that.

Not that money meant very much to Shamus Magee. He had never had enough of it to be familiar with the full force of its charm, and his personal wants were few. What he actually prized was his freedom.

He was not afraid of work, but the urge to go hunting or fishing, or merely to see the far side of some distant hill would suddenly come over him with compelling force. At such times he preferred to be free to travel without having to consider the inconvenience his action might cause some employer.

For this reason he seldom held a steady job, although he could command top wages from any of the big outfits. Instead he chose to work a few weeks at a time, breaking out a string of horses, and then move on to another ranch.

He was, he admitted without sorrow, a saddle tramp. Most people used the term disparagingly, but he wore his label with pride. He was his own boss, owing nothing to anyone. He had two horses, a good saddle, three extra shirts, a blanket roll and a slicker. What else could a man want beside guns? And he had guns, two matched Colts which had cost him three months' wages, and a rifle he would not trade for any other in the Park.

He loved guns in the same way he loved horses. Nobody had ever been able to outshoot him in any of the contests, yet he took pride in the fact that he had yet to draw a gun on a man in anger.

Not even on Calder, he thought, and grinned. He had the impulse to sing again. He liked to sing, and it would annoy his partner. But he did not. Another twenty-four hours and the horses would be sold and they could part — if not as friends, at least without any real bitterness between them. The prospect increased his carefree feeling and he hummed softly to himself. It would be good to be in town again, to see someone other than the sour-faced Mushy, to laugh with people and hear them laugh in return.

2

Belmont stood on the bank of the stream from which it drew its name, a collection of some three hundred buildings which had been erected according to the builders' fancies with small regard to the overall pattern of the town.

Only the main thoroughfare could truly be called a street. The others twisted and turned between the buildings as if they had been laid out by wandering livestock. They were alleys, little more than wheel tracks in the dust.

At sunset, Shamus and Mushy pushed their animals into the pole corral behind the Lobert Livery. They dropped bars in place and drew long, slow breaths of relief. Half broken horses are tricky and the stallion had been acting up.

Behind them, Claude Burton of the Bar

X rode his horse out of the rear door of the runway, hesitated for an instant and then pulled to the corral.

"Where'd you get the grey?" he asked.

"Where do you think?" Mushy Calder growled.

Claude Burton owned the biggest ranch in the territory. He was a big man, too, near middle age, with a hard mouth and chalky eyes. "When I ask a decent question I expect a decent answer, wolfer. He looks like a horse of mine that disappeared five or six years back."

"He ain't that old."

"I'll give you fifty dollars for him."

Calder's laugh was an insult in itself. He said, "Look, Mr. Burton," and his use of the "mister" only increased the insult. "That horse will bring two hundred if he brings a cent."

"Not from me."

"He ain't for sale to you."

Shamus Magee clucked disapprovingly. He had no love for the domineering owner of the Bar X. He had broken a number of horses for the outfit and Burton had always acted as if the world belonged to him and he had a fence around it. But Magee had no desire to see a fight start, and here was one a-building. He knew the signs.

"Wait a minute," he said. "You've got no call to act this way, Mushy. Claude asks a civil question and you answer like a bear with a sore paw. 'Course the horse is for sale, but not for fifty dollars. Why, I'd give more than that myself." He laughed at his own joke, the sound growing weaker as he realized that neither Burton nor Calder had joined in.

Burton just stared harder at Calder. He said, "Keep off my range, wolfer. That's an order." Then he swung his horse around so abruptly that the animal half stumbled, and spurred down the alley. Magee looked after him in dismay, then turned to his partner.

"I swear to God, Mushy, I never saw your beat. You'd rather have enemies than friends. I guess you'd quarrel with an angel just for exercise."

"Burton ain't no angel."

"Never said he was. But he might have bought some horses if you hadn't riled him. Maybe you'd better let me handle the selling end of this here business."

"Not to Burton you don't. I wouldn't give him a drink of water if I knew it was pure alkali."

Shamus had the unfamiliar impulse to hit a man. He resisted it, muttered, "See you in the morning," and moved away. But he did

16

not head for the saloons. All he wanted was a bath, a meal not of his own cooking, and a loss of memory in regard to his partnership with Mushy Calder. Afterward, he wanted to sleep.

He slept, long and soundly, until he had a dream. It was beautiful at first, a dream about timber and blue sky and the biggest elk he had ever had his sights on. But suddenly the elk charged. The rifle jammed. Next instant he was on the ground, the elk prancing on him with its sharp hoofs.

He woke, yelling, and found himself on the floor beside his bed, tangled in his blankets. He fought free and stood up and saw Mushy Calder.

"Where'd you come from?"

Calder shook his head. "I swear," he said, "you sleep like you was dead."

Shamus sat down. "Did you roll me out of bed?"

"How else was I going to get you to wake up?"

"I should bust you." Shamus gathered the blankets together with one hand. "Go away. I've got me an elk to shoot. Never missed one before in my life." He prepared to lie down again.

Calder squinted at him as if Shamus had lost his mind. "What are you talking about?"

"Nothing you'd understand." Shamus pounded the pillow back into shape. "Bet you never had a dream in your life. Me, I've had some fine ones. Even found a gold mine once."

Calder grunted. "It ain't no dream that the corral fence is busted and our horses gone," he said. "I just come from there."

Shamus Magee had just stretched out, full length. He sat up abruptly. "Say that again."

"The hostler says it happened about two o'clock. Said the racket waked him, and by the time he got outside the horses had kicked the fence apart and taken off."

Shamus got rid of the entangling blankets and came to his feet. "Kicked that fence down? I don't believe it."

"Neither do I." Calder's voice was suddenly savage. "Go down and have a look for yourself. I even found ax marks where they chopped out two posts."

Magee gulped. "Why would anybody do that?"

"Not anybody. Claude Burton. Didn't you see his eyes when he looked at that grey?"

Shamus sat down again slowly. He wiggled his toes. For some reason he always seemed to think more clearly when he was free to wiggle his toes. "Burton's no horse thief."

"Listen." Calder's voice rasped like a file

against hard metal. "Claude Burton never broke a law when he thought it might catch up with him, but he's mean and you know it. I could tell you a dozen stories, like the one when he burned out that homesteader on Cow Creek, or the time he bought up old Martin's mortgage and threw him out. How many ranches are left in the north end?"

Shamus did not say anything.

"And these horses. They weren't branded. They was wild when we roped them and if they got away by themselves and someone rounded them up who would they belong to?"

Shamus considered. It was a nice point of law, and one he could not answer.

"Look at it this way." Calder's small eyes narrowed wolfishly. "Supposing Burton caught those wild horses in the first place, and then they got away from him, and you caught them again. Wouldn't you figure maybe they belonged to you?"

"Seems as if I'd have some claim," Shamus said slowly.

"So the difference lies in the fact them horses didn't hightail it by themselves. They was helped, but how in hell are you going to prove it? I'll bet all the bounty money I earn next season that right now, at this minute, that grey stallion is at the Bar X and already wearing a Bar X brand."

"If he is it's a real dirty trick."

"That's what I expected you to say." Calder's tone was heavy with disgust. "A real dirty trick. Question is, what are you going to do about it?"

"Well, what can a man do? I guess maybe I could ride out and shoot Burton, but that seems to be going a little far over a horse."

Calder spat on the floor. "I might have known. You're too lazy to fight and Burton knows it. Why did I take you with me in the first place? Why didn't I team up with Tim Younger? No one would take a horse from Tim. He'd ride right up to the Bar X and make Burton eat that grey chunk by chunk."

Shamus started to say that maybe this was partly Calder's fault, that if the wolfer hadn't annoyed Burton on the night before none of this might have happened. He didn't. After all, it would not excuse Burton, if Burton had taken the horses.

He shrugged and the gesture seemed to increase Calder's anger. "You may be willing to lay down without a fight, but I'm not. I'm going to get that horse." He turned and jerked open the door.

"Wait a minute." Shamus went after him. "You'll just get yourself killed."

"The hell I will. I know a couple of things about Burton that you don't."

He was gone, slamming the door behind him.

Shamus went back and sat down on the bed and wiggled his toes thoughtfully. He didn't know just what to do, but finally decided that the best thing was to let Calder cool off for a while. Talking to the little man in his present aroused state would be a waste of time.

He rose and dressed and went downstairs in search of breakfast. After he finished he walked over, to the livery to see the damage for himself. There could be no doubt about it — the horses had not broken free by themselves. The posts had been chunky logs nearly a foot thick, and the poles which ran horizontally between the posts were thicker than Shamus' upper arm.

Nor had the men who had done it made any real effort to conceal their work. The posts had been chopped nearly through before they were broken off jaggedly at the ground level, and one of the poles had been dragged almost twenty feet along the alley. It was plain that the raiders held both him and Calder in contempt, almost daring them to do something about it.

Shamus turned away. No use talking to

the night hostler. The man could not have helped hearing the racket and rushing out to see what was going on. He might force the man to admit he was lying, but what was the use unless he meant to take action after that? As he had told Mushy, it hardly seemed worthwhile killing anybody over a horse.

He did not start to worry about Calder until late that afternoon. By that time the story had spread all over town. Every place he went he ran into veiled remarks about grey horses, half grins and queries as to how much he had made in the last five weeks.

Shamus enjoyed a joke as well as the next man. He had schooled his temper over the years until he had it under almost complete control. But by four o'clock he felt that he had had enough and retreated to the Belmont Bar. There he poured his troubles into the ear of his friend, Sam Goth.

"What do these fools want me to do, ride out to the Bar X and start a private war? Even if I felt like shooting Burton, which I don't, he's got twenty men who wouldn't be just standing around while I did the deed."

Goth filled a shot glass for him. "Take it easy, Shamus. I ain't seen you so worked up in a dozen years."

"I'm not worked up," Shamus said, not touching the liquor. "But they're as bad as Mushy Calder. He was prancing around my room before I woke up this morning, trying to start me out on the warpath. Which reminds me, I ain't seen his ugly face since."

"He rode out," Goth said, "about nine this morning. I seen him when I was opening up."

"Which way was he headed?"

"North."

"The fool's just crazy enough to try to get that horse back, Sam."

"I told you not to get mixed up with him, Shamus. If it was me, I'd get my horse and ride out of the country for a spell, heading south. Can't tell what will come of this. I've heard of feuds which went on for years that started over something less."

Shamus looked at him in surprise. "You saying I ought to run away? What would everybody in town think?"

"What do you care what they think? Actually most of them like you and they don't like Burton much, but that isn't the reason they're egging you on. They're just a bunch of ghouls, that's what they are. They like trouble, when it's happening to someone else, like people watching a prize fight."

Shamus knew that this was true. Still, they

23

were his friends for all their jibes and this was his town. Down deep, so deep that it seldom extruded through his coating of good nature, Shamus had a stubborn streak.

But he did not want to quarrel with Sam. He did not like quarreling with anyone, and Sam was about the best friend he had.

For that reason he left the bar and started up the street. A minute later he wished he hadn't. He stopped. He glanced back across his shoulder at the safety offered by the saloon door, but it was too far away.

A small figure had come out of Gunther's store and planted herself directly in his path.

"Hello, you horseless horseman."

He sighed, knowing from experience that there was no escape from Marty Clare. She would have her say even if she chased him back into the saloon to say it.

She was his cross, the burr beneath his saddle blanket, the bane of his existence. At times it seemed to him that she lived for no other reason than to goad him, that she sat up nights filing her small red tongue to give it a sharper edge.

He dismissed the idea of flight. Marty Clare had no inhibitions: She would think nothing of trailing him into a saloon or racing madly down the center of the main street with the speed of a young antelope, shrieking his name at every step.

He stood there wondering if she would ever grow up and become gentle and lady-like. This had been going on since she was twelve, for nearly six years. Six years . . . why, she was grown up, except that she neither showed nor acted her age.

She made her own rules, followed her own whims, galivanting around the country with the abandonment of an unbroken filly.

For years her behavior had caused talk. People said it was a shame her mother was dead and that poor Dr. Clare was too busy to oversee his daughter's upbringing. In fact the town's concern had reached such a point two years back that the good women of the community had formed themselves into a committee which called upon the doctor with the joyous news that his worries were over — they had found a nice, quiet foster home for the neglected girl where she would be disciplined properly and raised as a young lady should be.

The doctor had examined them, peering over his square, steel rimmed spectacles much as he might have peered at some new and interesting germ.

His face was sardonic, his dark eyes mocking, his crown of curly black hair unruly as usual. "Ladies," he had said, "I thank you, but unfortunately Marty and I cannot avail ourselves of your generous offer. If we did there might be a fair chance that she would grow up to be like one of you. God forbid that any such tragedy should happen. If I ever see such signs in her development, I'll shoot her. Now, get the hell out of my house and your noses out of my affairs. The only interest I want from any of you is the interest on the unpaid bills which some of you have owed me for too long."

The bachelors and even some of the married men laughed about it in the saloons. No doubt about it, the doc was a card, a real whirltailed sidewinder who didn't care who he bawled out when he got roused. And the girl was like him, wild as a sand flea and just as annoying.

The peppery physician, for all that he had attended nearly every family in the big valley at one time or another, was still a mystery, an outsider. He had arrived six years ago, with his daughter, to take over the practice of the old doctor who had just died. Where he came from or how he heard of the vacancy the valley did not know, nor had they asked. They were too relieved to have a doctor of any kind in that empty land.

Shamus looked at her mildly. Her red hair was too long to be worn loose, and too short to be gathered into a proper knot at the back of her head. Her face would have beauty if it ever filled out, but it was still thin. The spray of freckles across her slightly snubbed nose gave her an elfin quality and little green flecks danced in her gray eyes. Shamus saw recklessness in those eyes, and a veiled mockery, as if she were laughing at life and the people around her, sharing the joke only with her personal inner devil.

"What do you want now?" Shamus asked.

She planted both small fists on her hips. She wore no hat and the man's shirt, cut down to fit her, and the levis tucked into half boots, certainly did not constitute a proper costume for a nearly grown woman.

"I want to know what you're going to do," she said. "The whole town is laughing at you."

"Let them laugh."

"Shamus Magee. Do you mean to stand there and tell me you're going to let them steal those horses and not raise one little finger to get them back?"

"I'm not right sure that anyone stole them."

"I am. I saw them."

Shamus had not expected this.

"And I followed them, almost to the Bar X. They let the rest of the string go but the grey is at the ranch."

"Marty," he said, "you shouldn't be riding around like that at night, alone."

"Why not? I can take care of myself." She touched the grip of the thirty-two she wore in a holster. "I'm not like some people I know. I'm not afraid of a fight."

"My, you're warlike." He made it sound admiring.

"And you're not. You wear two guns, low down, like some badman from the Nations, and all you ever shoot at is jackrabbits."

He laughed. He couldn't help it. She was so mad.

"Go ahead and laugh," she said bitterly. "You're a great big joke, and all you do is laugh. If you were the man I used to love you'd go out there and get that horse and rub old Burton's nose in the dirt."

"So you don't love me any more? That is a relief."

"And that's not funny either, because I really and truly was going to marry you until this happened. But when I get me a man I want one who can fight, one who doesn't have to crawl around like a whipped dog, licking the boots of anyone who kicks him."

For some reason, perhaps because he had been enduring jeers all day, the girl's words got under Shamus' skin. Usually he brushed her barbs away as he would a buzzing fly, but now he reached out and caught her thin shoulders between his hands.

"You listen to me once, Marty Clare. You're nothing but a fool kid, babbling about love, babbling about bravery, blabbing, blabbing, blabbing. I've let you call me names for years, but you're getting too old to act this way. It's time you grew up. Now, I'm going to tell you something I never told anyone else, and if you repeat it I'll bust your back side until you can't set a saddle for a month. You talk about killers, and being brave, and you don't know what you're saying. You never saw a killer in your life, but I did. My father wore two guns and he didn't use them for jackrabbits. I was six the night he came home and I heard him and my mother talking. He'd just killed another man.

"I heard Ma give a little cry, like no other sound I'd ever heard her make before, all full of hopelessness. 'That's the third one, Jack. The third man.'

"He came back at her then, sour-like, quarreling. 'What do you want me to do, just stand there and get shot without fighting back?'

" 'Better that,' she said, and she sounded worn out. 'Better that than turn into a professional killer. Sometimes it takes more courage to avoid a fight than to get into one.'

"I didn't hear anything more, but it scared me, the way Pa slammed out of the house. At midnight Ma picked me up and we went down to the station and got on the train. I never saw my father again."

He released her, then, for two tears had appeared unexpectedly in Marty Clare's eyes. She shut her lids to try to stop them, but they forced their way through her long lashes and ran down the swell of her cheeks.

"Why did you never tell me, Shamus?"

Shamus gaped at her in open-mouthed consternation. He had never seen Marty Clare cry before. "Stop it," he said.

"And I called you a coward."

"Guess maybe I am."

"No you're not. You're brave and sweet and I'll marry you after all, just as soon as I come back from school."

He started. The threat of marriage did not bother him. She had been making it from almost the first day they had met. But he said, "What's this about school?"

"My father says I have to go next fall. He says I'm growing up like a young wildcat."

"He's sure right about that."

"He says there's a school way back East

where they will knock the rough edges off of me."

"God help them."

"So I've got to go, but I'll come back. I didn't care much when I thought you were a coward, but now I know how brave you are and I'm not sure I want to go."

He said hastily, "You go. Your pa is right. There's a lot of things a girl like you has to learn." He turned and made his escape, back into the saloon, and for once Marty Clare did not follow him.

3

The week that followed was one of the worst Shamus could remember. The story about the vanished horses was all over the country. It just seemed to grow and grow.

Twice he decided that he could stand it no longer. Twice he prepared to pull out, and both times a sly remark, once by the livery owner and the second by the hotel clerk, caused him to stay.

He sat at a rear table in the Belmont Bar, nursing his growing resentment, avoiding conversation whenever possible until Sam Goth grew concerned about him.

"I swear," Sam said, "I never saw such difference in a human in all my life. If I didn't know better I'd figure you'd changed minds with Mushy Calder."

Shamus growled at him. "I'm beginning to believe Mushy's right. Ain't one of these busybodies got nothing to do besides pester me?"

"That's the trouble with the human race," Dr. Clare's voice said. He had come in through the bar's rear door so quietly that neither Sam nor Shamus had noticed him.

Sam Goth said, "Hi, Doc."

The doctor did not trouble to return the greeting. He walked over to the table and sat down, facing Shamus. "You're just finding out," he said, "that most men are coyotes and that they'd sacrifice even their friends for a poor joke."

Unbidden, Sam came around the bar, bringing a bottle of whiskey and a glass which he set before Clare. "If that's the way you feel about them, Doc, I wonder you go to all the bother to save as many as you do."

Clare steepled a dark eyebrow. He was a handsome man of fifty, but his features often assumed a Satanic cast.

"That's a question I've asked myself for years, Sam. We all in our own way are slaves to habit, or custom, or a senseless thing we call duty. Supposing you get sick, supposing I let you die. You are, after all, a rather worthless human being."

Goth grinned, a little uncomfortably.

"So worthless," Clare said, "that I wouldn't want you on my conscience. For that reason, and for that alone, I'd do my best to prolong your existence." He poured himself a drink and downed it neatly.

"As for you, Shamus. No man with his full reason doubts your courage, or the fact that you are generally loved. But curiously people delight in picking on people they love. Observe my daughter for example. She has professed love for you almost from the instant she laid eyes on your hulking form."

It was Shamus' turn to be uncomfortable. He had not known that anyone was conscious of Marty's intense interest in him.

"Ah, she's just a kid, Doc. She's talking through her hat."

The doctor smiled a devil's smile at him. "If I hadn't felt certain you would react that way I'd have shot you long ago, Shamus. Some men might have taken this wordy passion seriously and attempted to turn it to their advantage. But I trust you, Shamus, although I frankly have no desire to see you as a son-in-law."

"Don't worry. I never had such an idea."

"Probably not, but you still have certain things to learn about women, and especially about Marty. Up until this point she has merely been talking. With her it was an idea to be played with as a cat toys with a mouse.

"She learned early that her references to her love annoyed you, so she continued them — but after this week I'm not so sure."

Shamus blinked uneasily. "Maybe what you're saying makes some kind of sense, Doc."

"It does," Clare assured him. "The other day you aroused her sympathy. You told her a story about a gunman."

Shamus' face took on a slight reddish tinge. "I told her if she repeated it I'd spank her bottom."

"My daughter seldom fails to tell me things. But to continue. You aroused her sympathy and that is a dangerous thing to do with a woman. Get them feeling sorry for you, and the rest is usually easy. For that reason I wish she were leaving for school tommorrow. I should have sent her away last year or the year before, but I am human and also lonesome. I kept her by me as long as I could."

He rose, making a kind of small, stiff-necked bow. "Goodbye, gentleman." He made a right about turn which would have done credit to an Army officer and walked to the door. Not until it had closed gently behind him did Shamus and the bartender look at each other.

"Well," Shamus said, "maybe you can tell me what that was all about."

Sam Goth wiped his face with a corner of his apron. He used the doctor's glass to pour himself a drink and downed it before he said, "I'd judge that he was warning you to keep away from his kid, and if I was you I'd do just that. There are a lot of men I'd rather have sore at me than Doc. He's one of the most dangerous people I ever knew."

It was getting dark when Shamus left the bar and walked the two blocks to the frame hotel. The wind had come up, chasing dust and litter ahead of him as he moved slowly along the board sidewalk.

Life, he thought with growing bitterness, was certainly getting complicated. First the grey horse and now Marty Clare. He wished he had never heard of either of them.

He came into the lobby to find the long room in semidarkness, the big overhead lamps as yet unlighted, and went to the desk to get his key. Harvey Modge was behind the desk working on his ledger.

Harvey was old and nearly toothless, and his pointed chin and sharp nose seemed to come almost together like the jaws of a nutcracker, separated only by his sunken cheeks.

"Woman to see you." His old eyes were bright with curiosity

For an instant the only woman Shamus could think of was Marty Clare. He fought down an impulse to run. Then he turned slowly. She rose from the shadowed chair in the far corner.

His first reaction was that she was a stranger, someone he had never seen before. His second was that she was beautiful. His third was a deep curiosity.

He moved to meet her, lowering his voice, hoping that the conversation would not carry to Modge's flapping ears. "You wanted to see me?"

"If you're Shamus Magee."

"I'm right certain of that." He smiled, but he saw no relaxation in the tight level line of her full mouth. She drew a folded slip of paper from her pocket and held it toward him. He took it uncertainly, still watching her face, still trying to guess who she was and why she was here. Then he dropped his eyes to the note and read the cramped, backhand scrawl:

I got something to show you, and jobs for both of us. Miss Dodge will tell you about it. Come running.

Mushy.

He read it twice, surprised, for he had never known that Mushy could read or write. Then he looked up to find the girl studying him.

"You're Miss Dodge?"

"Myra Dodge."

"And what is this mystery of Mushy's?"

"Mushy tells me you hate Claude Burton."

That startled him. He wanted to say, "You've got it wrong, Miss. I don't hate Burton. I never hated anyone in my life." But his curiosity was very strong, and he was very conscious of her nearness and the faint perfume she used.

"Well, let's say I don't like him much."

"I shouldn't think you would, after he stole your horses."

Shamus did not answer and after a moment she went on. "I'm looking for men, men I can trust, men who are not afraid to stand up to Burton."

"Uh-huh."

"I'll pay well, and I'll protect you, and I'll see that everyone gets a bonus when it's over."

"When what's over?"

"When Burton's been run out of the country or is dead."

He was jarred by that. She did not look like the type who would want anyone dead. Her hair was a warm blond, her eyes blue, her face very pretty, almost soft. But her mouth was a determined line and her voice sounded a little husky, as if from deep feeling.

He thought, I've never seen anyone like her in my life. Her clothes had obviously not been bought in Belmont, but they weren't flashy. They were rich looking as if they had cost a great deal of money at one of the country's better stores.

Aloud he said, "I'm afraid you've made a mistake. Mushy ought to know better than to send you on an errand like this. He knows I'm not much of a fighter."

"He said you weren't, until you got stirred up."

Shamus grinned. "And did he tell you that I seldom if ever get stirred up?"

"Even when your horses are stolen? I thought that in this country there wasn't anything anyone hated worse than a horse thief."

"Well, I guess that's right, but then, this was kind of a peculiar case. You see, those horses didn't belong to anyone until we

38

brought them in, and if we'd branded them probably no one would have touched them. But we figured on selling them right away so we didn't go to the trouble."

"And you think that excuses Burton for what he did?"

Shamus shook his head.

"And you're going to take it lying down?"

"Well, what can I do about it unless I kill him? Did you ever kill a man, Ma'am?"

"Of course not, but —"

"Well, I didn't either, and somehow I feel right good about not getting started. I —" He broke off. The lobby door had slammed open and three men had trailed into the room. He would have paid no attention to them except for the change in the girl's expression. He watched her, fascinated. She was no longer beautiful. Her lips seemed to flatten and her eyes widen. If he had ever seen fear he was seeing it now. He started to turn toward the men but the leader shoved him aside roughly.

"Get out of the way, Shamus."

He took two steps to regain his balance. He swung around and recognized Budlong Cole and two of the Bar X hands. He said, "Now wait a minute, Bud," but Cole paid no attention to him. It was as if Cole knew there was no danger in Shamus Magee, knew that no matter what happened Shamus would not fight. Cole stopped before the girl, a tall man, powerfully built, a hard man with the reputation of doing anything that Claude Burton ordered.

"You were told not to come to town," he said. "Go get your horse and ride out. Dutch will see that you get back to the ranch safe."

"I'm not going."

She might be scared to death, Shamus thought in admiration, but the fear did not reach her voice.

"You're going." Cole spoke to her as he would to an unruly child. "You can walk out of here nice and ladylike, or we'll tie you up and toss you in a buckboard. The choice is yours."

Shamus had never heard anyone use that tone to a woman, especially one who was so evidently a lady. He said, "Wait a minute, Bud," and Cole said, "Keep out of this." He said it as if he simply could not waste time on Shamus Magee. "I'll take care of you later," he added absently.

Something happened to Shamus Magee. Finally something happened.

"You'll take care of me now," he said, and took a step forward.

"Dutch. Henry." Cole glanced at the two

men who had followed him into the lobby, and they understood. They closed in on either side of Shamus Magee. They had known Magee a long time. Neither bothered to touch his gun.

Henry was closest. Shamus hit him. The blow traveled less than six inches but it landed squarely on the point of Henry's long jaw. Henry sat down, swayed, and fell over on his face.

Dutch paused for just an instant. Then with a muttered curse he jumped on Shamus' back. The next instant he was flying across the lobby, turning over completely in the air. He crashed against the lobby wall, slid down to the floor and stayed there.

Cole swung around. He stood looking at Shamus as if he did not believe it, and then he grinned with a kind of hungry, savage joy. No man in the whole valley loved a fight for fighting's sake more than Bud Cole.

"You asked for it," he said, and crouched a little, his arms seeming to dangle almost to the floor. He had a long face made sinister by a thin knife scar which started at the left corner of his mouth and ran up to a point directly before the ear. "Come get me, boy!"

Shamus Magee watched him. Cole was said to be the best barroom fighter this side of the hills. The man weighed a good two hundred pounds, and none of it was fat. His hands were big and his arm muscles filled his shirtsleeves.

Magee moved in. A long arm shot out of nowhere to crash against the side of his head, spinning him half around. A second fist jarred into his body, driving him backward toward the wall.

He stood there shaking his head, trying to clear it, watching as Cole stalked him. Then he charged, the force of his rush coupled with his weight carrying him through the barrage of blows which Cole threw at him. He had his head down, protecting his chin with his shoulder as he bored in. He got close enough to wrap his big arms about Cole and they stood for an instant straining against each other, testing their respective strengths, before they went down together in a crashing fall which shook the entire building.

Shamus fell on top but Cole rolled at once, taking Shamus with him. They pounded at each other's sides, grunting and writhing, then broke free.

Shamus was the first on his feet. His years of breaking horses had taught him to rise quickly from a fall. He was upright before Cole found his footing, and he had the moment to set himself before he sent the long, overhand right crashing against the Bar X foreman's temple.

Cole went down. He sat groggily for a full minute and then he reached for his gun.

Shamus saw the motion. It never occurred to him to draw his own weapon. He simply took a step forward and kicked the man's wrist.

Cole's half drawn gun slid across the floor. Cole cried out sharply, shrilly, and twisted away, grabbing his numbed wrist with his other hand. Shamus waited, panting. He tasted salt in his mouth, a taste that meant blood was leaking from a cut lip. His face was puffy and battered, but for some reason he couldn't stop grinning.

"Get up," he said.

Cole stared at him.

"Get up." He drew his gun, not because he thought he needed it but because the fight had gone far enough and he wanted to discourage Cole from starting it over again.

Cole rose slowly, still nursing the damaged wrist, his eyes burning slits in his narrow face.

"Get the others up." Shamus indicated Dutch and Henry both of whom were beginning to stir.

Cole walked over and kicked Henry in the

side. The man groaned and sat up.

"On your feet," Cole said.

He rose slowly. Shamus took two steps and lifted the gun from Henry's holster. Then he backed to where Dutch had dragged himself to his knees and added another gun to his collection.

"Now get your horses and ride out."

They watched him. Cole said, "Better use that gun now, Shamus."

Shamus blinked at him.

"Use it while you can," Cole said. "I'll kill you the next time we meet."

He stalked to the door, stepping out into the darkness. Dutch and Henry stood as if rooted to the spot, then suddenly both turned at once and broke for the opening, shouldering each other in their haste to escape. Shamus looked at the gun in his hand. He looked at it as if he had never seen it before.

4

Shamus Magee rode north with Myra Dodge beside him. When he thought about it he wondered exactly what had happened to him. The girl was like no one he had ever met before.

Myra Dodge had wanted many things in

her life and had been willing to trade to get them. One thing she understood above all others. Men.

Not that she had ever prostituted herself. She was much too clever for that. Her good looks and blond softness masked a steel-trap mind, capable of turning almost any situation to her advantage.

Only one man in her whole experience had proved as hard, as grasping and as ruthless as she. That man, Claude Burton, she hated thoroughly, hated for having seen through her mask, hated for having laughed at her.

She thought grimly now: I'll teach Burton something he's never learned. I'll teach him that he can't turn me down, can't laugh at me. No one in this country dares stand against the old pirate. He's bullied and scared everyone on the range, chased them out, robbed them, cheated them. But he will not cheat me.

She felt no sympathy for the people Burton had victimized. She had no patience with weakness of any kind, and the very fact that she was a woman born angered her. Had she been a man she would have asked odds of no one, but as a woman she needed help in the battle ahead.

She had to use her charm to entice men

to her cause. She was using it on Shamus Magee now, Magee whom she regarded with a certain contempt. Physically he was a magnificent animal, and it had stirred her to watch the seeming ease with which he had handled the Bar X riders. But she knew that he would always have to be goaded into a fight, that he would not be a ready weapon in her hands.

This did not daunt her in the least. She had broken down stronger men than Magee, and she meant to call on every trick, every device she knew to bind him to her side.

"I feel terrible," she said, "getting you into all this trouble. That Cole, he's a monster."

Shamus Magee had never thought of Budlong Cole as a monster. He did not like the big Bar X foreman any better than he liked Claude Burton, but in all fairness he recognized that both were capable cattlemen. Some of their methods did not jibe with his way of doing things, but still, he had never set himself as a judge of other men's actions.

"He'll kill you the next time he sees you," Myra Dodge said.

"So I'll try not to see him."

"You're running away?" Her voice was

incredulous. "A man like you, running away?"

Shamus stirred uneasily in his saddle. For some reason he wanted this girl's good opinion above all else. It puzzled him. Two hours ago he had never even heard of her.

He ran a hand over his bruised cheek reflectively. She was the most important thing in his world. Shamus admitted to himself that he knew very little about love. He had regarded most women as nuisances. Not that he didn't enjoy dancing or appreciate the sight of a pretty girl, but he had spent so much of his range-roving life alone or among men that he viewed the few women he met with a kind of embarrassed suspicion. He could not talk to them freely as he could to a man.

Myra Dodge was different. In the five minutes it had taken to bathe the blood from his face and put a bandage over the cut at his temple, she had told him more about herself than he had ever known about any other woman.

"It's not a pretty story," she said. "My uncle owned the Diamond D. I didn't know him very well. I've been living in Denver, but this spring he came to see me. He said he was having trouble with a man named Burton. He said he couldn't stay in the

47

country any longer because Burton would kill him. He also told me Burton wouldn't attack a woman. He offered to sell me the ranch for four thousand dollars."

Shamus had listened, not surprised. It fitted Burton's reputation.

"So, I bought it. I was raised on a small place in the southern part of the state. I know something about cattle and I figured all I had to do was to get a crew and run the place. I didn't expect persecution from Burton. Men don't usually pick on a woman."

Shamus made a small noise in his throat and she glanced at him, gauging the effect of her words.

"But I had trouble hiring a crew, a few riders from up by Hawthorn. Burton immediately ran them off."

Shamus wondered how much she knew about the old mining camp of Hawthorn, and the brush outlaws who made it their headquarters. Certainly if she had intended trouble with Burton she could not have chosen a better way to start it than to hire those rustlers. He almost said so, but he waited to hear the rest.

"Well, that wasn't the worst. In a few days Burton rode over to see me. He told me a woman like me shouldn't be living alone, and that there was a place for me at his ranch."

Shamus stiffened.

"Oh, he offered to marry me." She added this last because pride would not let her admit that she could not get any man in the world if she wanted him. "I laughed in his face, and the next thing I knew he sent Bud Cole and three men to take me by force to the Bar X."

Shamus was suddenly very angry, more angry than he could recall being in his whole life. "Someone should hang him. Did he —"

She shook her head. "He locked me in that cabin at the back of the main meadow. He said I was to stay there until I got some sense. I'd still be there if Mushy hadn't let me out."

Shamus showed his surprise. "Mushy?"

She nodded. "I saw him yesterday morning, just at daybreak. He was scouting around, looking for that grey horse, and I recognized him. He'd gotten some wolves on my range earlier this spring.

"I called to him from the window and he rode over. They had a chain on the door and heavy strips nailed across the window, but he used his rope and pulled two strips loose with his horse. And then he took me back to the Diamond D."

"Where is he now?"

"Back in the hills, looking for men to hire. But he told me about you. He said you were one of the best men in the valley, that you had more friends than anyone he knew, and that if I could get you on my side, why, not a rider in the valley would hesitate to come to work for me."

She finished the bandage and stepped back, examining the result critically. "That will do."

"Look," Shamus said. "We should go to the sheriff. Even Burton can't get away with grabbing a woman and locking her up like that. Why, the sheriff will have him in jail in an hour."

"No."

He stared at her.

"You've got to promise me that you won't tell the sheriff, that you won't tell anyone what I told you. Promise."

"But why?"

"You great big goose. Don't you realize how much talk there would be if anything like this came out?"

"I know Burton would be in a lot of trouble."

"You don't understand," she said. "You're a gentleman, and you'd never believe anything bad about a woman. But I'm a stranger in this country. I live alone and if this ever got out Burton would have to defend himself. Do you know what kind of stories he'd tell, and his crew would tell?"

Shamus nodded helplessly.

"So you see, I can't go to the sheriff. All I can do is go back to the ranch and hope that Mushy has managed to hire some men."

"Alone?"

She glanced at him sidewise. "Looks that way."

"But you can't. What if Bud Cole and his men are waiting for you along the trail?"

"That's a chance I have to take."

"All right," Shamus said. "I'll go with you."

She shook her head. "No, you mustn't. I've already caused you trouble enough. You owe me nothing."

He wanted to tell her suddenly that he owed her everything, that before he'd seen her he had not known what it was to be alive. "A man's got to fight for something," he said. "A man has to fight when he wants something. Maybe I never wanted anything bad enough before."

He did not see the secret smile, because she had turned away. But he did see her shoulders straighten, and he noticed a certain confidence in her from that time on. She had won again.

5

The Diamond D was not much of a ranch. Shamus Magee had ridden by it several times, but he had never bothered to turn in to the long track which led back to the collection of squared log buildings. Nor had he known Myra Dodge's uncle except to speak to. Dodge had been a bachelor, a grumpy man who lived alone with a couple of rag-tailed hands and ran some thousand head of cattle across the flats.

The trail went on after passing the ranch turnoff, twisting upward through Bright Canyon to reach the ancient buildings of Hawthorn.

Years ago, long lines of ore wagons had cut deep ruts in the rocky soil as they wound down to the smelter which had stood beside the Belmont. But the mines had played out, the ore wagons were gone. Only the traces left by their metal-rimmed wheels remained, and these were now grass-grown and at places even covered by brush. The trail north was seldom used by anyone except outlaws.

Shortly after sunup Shamus and Myra Dodge turned their tired horses into the lane and rode back toward the ranch. The weathered buildings looked deserted as they came around the corner of a hay shed and moved on to the corral.

Shamus had been watchful ever since they left the road. He had seen nothing that suggested immediate danger, yet he heaved a sigh of relief as he stepped from the saddle and offered the girl his hand. And then from the corner of his eye he caught movement beyond the house. He went tense, his big hand dropping on the stock of his holstered gun.

"What is it?" The girl twisted nervously in her saddle to see what had attracted his attention. Then she laughed, relief making the sound almost shrill. "It's Mushy."

Calder came around the corner of the house, small and bandy-legged and unimpressive. He was carrying a rifle and his battered hat rode the back of his little head.

"Just wanted to be sure it wasn't none of Burton's men after the grey."

"You mean you've got him?"

"Course. Got him last night. He's in a box canyon a couple of miles back in the hills. Didn't think I was going to let Burton get away with stealing him, did you?"

Shamus didn't say anything but his heart seemed to drop into the pit of his stomach. It wasn't fear, not personal fear. It was hopelessness. The last thing he wanted was a range war with Claude Burton. True, Burton needed to be punished. Horsewhipped might be the proper thing for what he'd done to Myra. But to take the grey out of the Bar X corral, that was almost a declaration of war.

The girl did not seem concerned. "Did you sign up any men?"

"Didn't try. I was busy with the grey. I had to cover the tracks, didn't I?"

"But you promised."

Calder spat in the dust. "Figured Shamus would bring a passel of his friends. Always bragging about how many friends he's got, Shamus is."

Magee felt his cheeks redden. Calder sure had a way of making a man dislike him. "How'd you know I'd come?"

Mushy Calder grinned wickedly. "Never had a doubt. This female can talk the warts off a toad. I figured she'd snare you one way or another."

Shamus took half a step toward him. "Some day, Mushy, I'm going to break you up like you deserve. Keep your tongue to yourself."

Calder brought the rifle around in a quick, decisive gesture. "Just keep coming, Shamus boy. You always did have too much wind in you."

"Stop it!" The girl swung down from her saddle. "What's the matter with you, Mushy? If you're so all fired set on a fight, save it for Burton."

"Aim to." Calder sounded unperturbed. "Just didn't want Mr. Shamus Magee thinking I'd back up for him or anyone else, that's all."

She said worriedly, "We've got to have a crew. You'd better get your horse and ride up to Hawthorn and see how you can make out. Offer them fifty and found with a bonus of fifty if they stay through September."

Shamus cut in. "Now wait a minute, Miss Myra. Before you go off half-cocked just let's do some figuring. First we don't need to make Burton madder than he already is. If I know Claude he's plenty hot under the collar. Not only do you escape him, but I beat up three of his men and Mushy stole a horse."

" 'Twasn't his horse," Mushy growled.

"Of course not." Shamus was trying to hold his patience. "But you know as well as I do, once he's laid a hand on anything he thinks it's his." As he said this he met

55

Myra's eyes, flushed, and quickly turned away.

"So if we bring any of them outlaws down from the hills," he concluded, "Burton is going to be really mad. He'll probably wind up hanging all of us."

"Well, we've got to get a crew."

Shamus took a long, slow breath. He still didn't quite understand how he'd gotten into this so deep, but he realized that he was in, clear up to his neck.

"Why don't I see if I can get you some regular riders, decent hands that Burton or anyone else can't squawk about? That way we won't stir up the other ranchers against us. If we put outlaws and gunmen on the payroll we'll wind up fighting not only Burton but the whole valley."

He was so occupied with his thinking, with trying to get his point across, that he did not see the quick look which passed between Mushy Calder and the girl. This scene had been carefully plotted between them, and Calder had never intended to seek help from the hills. They were forcing his hand, neatly, expertly, Calder as much from malice as anything, the girl to cause Shamus to do exactly what he was doing now.

"Do you think you can get them?"

He rubbed his puffed cheek, considering. "I hope so. Fifty is good wages, and the bonus sounds fine. I'll ride in tonight and try." He turned, intending to put their horses into the corral, then stopped. There was a long, tree studded draw a quarter of a mile south of the house and as he swung around his quick eye had caught movement in the draw. Without moving, without taking his eyes from the spot, he said sharply:

"Company. Mushy, fade back to the house, get on the roof if you can and cover the yard. But if you use that rifle before I yell I'll personally take the skin off your back and nail it to the barn. Mind now."

One thing about Calder. He might be the meanest, most disagreeable jasper in that part of the country, but he was a good woodsman and a crack shot. There was no one, Shamus felt as he watched the Bar X riders lift themselves from the draw and race toward the ranch, whom he would rather have covering him at a time like this.

He counted six riders in all, and even at the distance he had no difficulty recognizing the leaders — Claude Burton by his bulk, Bud Cole by his height.

"Better get in the house, Ma'am."

"I'll stay here."

Her voice was level, unhurried, unafraid.

Her eyes, following the newcomers as they swung into the lane, were a little narrow. Her lips had flattened until her mouth no longer looked soft and inviting. But Shamus was not watching her. He pulled the saddles and bridles off the horses as if he did not know there was anyone within a hundred miles of him, put the animals into the enclosure, fastened the gate and tossed the saddles on the fence. Then he turned, seeing the riders spread out a little into a kind of skirmish line and come on, slowing their pace to an uneven trot.

He stood loosely, one elbow resting on the top bar of the fence, a heel hooked over the lowest bar. It was an awkward position, one from which a man would have difficulty in drawing a gun, a peaceful position, nothing hostile about it. He could not have said more plainly that he neither wanted nor expected a fight — not unless he held both hands high in the air.

"Howdy."

Burton and Cole pulled up, reining their horses a little sidewise as though to corner Shamus and the girl against the fence. Their four men fanned out in a half circle behind them.

"I might have guessed you'd be here," Burton said.

Shamus' face was the picture of bland wonder. "Well now." He glanced at Cole, who was scowling at him, his dark face bearing livid marks of last night's fight. "Why shouldn't I be here? It's a free country. Or is it?"

Burton made a motion of his hand as if to wipe Shamus' words aside. "Where's the horse?"

"Horse?" Shamus' puzzlement seemed genuine. "What horse are you meaning, Claude?"

Burton was containing his obvious anger with difficulty. "You know damn well what horse I mean. That grey stallion. He was in the back pasture last night. He was gone this morning."

Shamus appeared to study the problem with care. "Maybe he got out," he suggested innocently. "If it's the horse I'm thinking of he has a right smart habit of getting loose. Did he kick the fence down?"

Burton seemed to swell. "The fence was cut and you know it. You've got just half an hour to turn over that horse and ride out of this country. I should hang you for monkeying with my fence."

"Look," Shamus said, and his voice had changed subtly. "Your friend Cole can tell you where I was last night. Him and me had a little argument. I couldn't be pounding in his head and taking a horse at the same time."

"And he was with me the rest of the night. We just got here." The girl took a step forward. Her hands were on her hips and she glared up at Burton. "You're on my land. I'll give you just five minutes to get off."

Burton barely glanced at her. "I'll talk to you in a minute."

"You'll talk to me now. For your information Magee is working for me. He's bringing in a crew from the south end of the valley and we're going to push the cattle back onto the grass you hazed them off of last week. Now get out."

"Let me take him, boss." It was Cole, his face hungry with hate. "I told the fool I'd kill him the next time we met."

"Quiet," Burton said. "I want that horse. If he turns it over, he rides out. What happens after that is your business. Come on, Shamus, you always acted before like you had sense. What's got into you?"

"Maybe I just got tired of being good natured while other men spit on me."

"All right," Burton said. "You asked for it. Put a rope on him boys."

One of the riders moved forward, shaking

60

out his rope. The rest watched Shamus like circled buzzards, seeming to pray that he would make a move toward his gun.

He lifted his voice. "Look at the house, you fools. Mushy watch it."

Their eyes shifted away from him. Calder stood on the house's flat roof, his rifle ready, his thin body bent a little forward.

"You all know Mushy." Shamus resumed his easy drawl. "Mushy ain't big, but he's the best shot with a rifle in the valley and he's rattlesnake mean. I'll bet he can get five of you before you can get me."

They sat motionless. The man who had been shaking out his rope just let it dangle. The girl laughed suddenly, jeeringly.

"The great Claude Burton! You're good at fighting women, Burton. Go ahead, pull your gun!"

Shamus wished she hadn't said that. He glanced at her almost in reproof. Of course he realized how she must feel, but it wasn't quite right to jeer at a man who was under a gun.

Burton's face was black. "You're all very smart," he said. "Well, open your party."

"No party," Shamus said, and came away from the fence. He moved with deliberate slowness, afraid that a sudden move might spook one of the nervous riders into going for his gun. "You know me, Burton. I don't like violence — never did like it — but I'm serving notice right now. You can't pick on women and get away with it."

"She's no woman, she's —"

Shamus Magee moved with incredible swiftness. He jumped the four feet which separated him from Burton, caught the surprised rancher by the leg and dumped him out of the saddle. Bud Cole moved convulsively and the rifle cracked from the house roof. The bullet notched Cole's hat brim and Calder's voice sent its warning flat across the yard. "Stay quiet. The next will be in your head."

They sat quiet, immobile in their saddles. Burton had landed on his back. He got up heavily. Shamus stood above him, watching him with an almost sleepy expression, a slight smile on his lips. And Claude Burton couldn't take that.

He charged, head down, like an enraged bull. Shamus stepped sidewise and used the edge of his hand to hit Burton in the back of the lowered head. The big man stumbled over Shamus' extended leg and plunged face down in the dirt, and above his grunt as the wind was driven out of him the girl's high, mocking laugh rose clear.

Shamus heard her. The sound again annoyed him, but he did not make the mistake of taking his eyes from Burton. The man lay there unmoving, as if he were dead; then slowly he hoisted himself to his hands and knees, and even more slowly to his feet.

"Had enough?" Shamus asked.

The rancher did not look at him. He turned and groped blindly for the saddle.

"Wait a minute."

Burton stopped. He stood, his back toward Shamus, his head bent a little forward.

"Lift your gun and let it slide in the dirt."

"Go to hell."

Shamus' voice suddenly cracked like a whip. No one had ever heard him speak that way before.

"You're a fool, Burton. You've been big dog on this range so long you've forgotten other people have rights and feelings. Well, you're going to learn different. We're here, and we're here to stay, and the first one of your men rides across Diamond D land or touches Diamond D stock gets hurt. Do you think I'm crazy enough to let you ride away with your guns so you can turn and smoke us out as soon as you get to the draw? Drop it or I'll take it away from you and shove it down your throat — your teeth with it, too."

No one in the yard doubted that he meant it.

"And after that," he said, "I'll put you all afoot and let you walk home."

Claude Burton lifted his hand carefully, raised his heavy gun and let it fall.

"Now get on your horse, Burton. The rest of you spill your guns, one at a time. You first, Cole." He had drawn his own. He stood ready, feet apart, raking them with his eyes.

They obeyed sullenly, and he knew he had made life-long enemies this morning. For some reason the thought did not disturb him. He felt nothing but contempt for these mounted men who had gloried in working for the Bar X, who had taken pleasure in hazing and tormenting the homesteaders and small ranchers surrounding the big ranch.

Burton mounted. In the saddle, dust stained, quiet, stolid, he seemed to make a speechless threat with every breath he took.

"Get out of here," Shamus said.

Burton wheeled his horse. His men fell in behind him. They tore out of the lane as if Calder were firing at them from the roof-top perch.

Shamus watched them go, poker-faced but very thoughtful. The die was cast. There could be no retreat now. Claude Burton would never forget what had happened this day.

He turned toward the girl. She was still looking after the Bar X riders as they galloped down the road. Finally she swung to face him.

"You were magnificent," she said.

Shamus would have been less than human if he had not enjoyed the praise.

Mushy Calder slid down from the roof.

"What about me?" he demanded.

She gave him her warm smile. "You too, Mushy. I could kiss you for the way you acted."

"Don't bother."

Shamus felt a touch of jealousy. She had not mentioned kissing him. "What do we do now?" he asked.

"Can you actually get us a crew?"

He hesitated, reviewing in his mind the men he knew. "I think so."

"Then I'll get some food. It might be wise to clean out the bunkhouse. I don't think Uncle Andrew was very careful about such things, judging by the way the main house looked."

He grinned. He had an idea from the outside that Andrew Dodge probably had not been the world's best housekeeper.

"Come on, Mushy."

Calder shook his head. "I got to go look at the grey. After all the trouble I've had with that horse I wouldn't want nothing to happen to him."

Shamus started to protest, then recalled that he preferred Calder's absence to his company. With a shrug he headed for the bunkhouse.

It was a log building with a low slant roof and a round-bellied stove in one corner. It contained bunks for ten men, although Shamus was certain that the ranch had never employed anywhere near that number.

The floor was caked with dirt, the whole place filthy. He got a broom, a mop and a bucket of water and went to work. After a while he forgot the fight, and the unpleasantness of the last few days. He began to sing:

The lonesomest cowboy
That ever was known
Ate garlic for breakfast
And rode all alone.

Without friend or partner
Or sweetheart so dear,
And even his horse made him
Mount from the rear.

He paused for breath and then attacked the job with renewed vigor, adding another verse.

He roamed the wide prairie,
His job was immense,
To keep on the go
And forever ride fence.

A voice from behind him said, "I never heard that song before. Where did it come from?"

He looked around to find Myra Dodge in the open doorway. His face felt hot.

"Shucks, it ain't nothing. Just some foolishness I made up."

"You mean you wrote it?"

"Well, it's not written down. I just sing it sometimes."

"Are there more verses?"

His embarrassment grew. "Honest, you wouldn't want to hear them."

"Go ahead. Sing it for me."

He didn't know quite what to do. Her eyes were smiling at him, and her lips looked soft and warm. He cleared his throat, singing in a voice more cracked than usual.

From line camp to line camp
Around and around,

And haze the stray dogies
Back on their home ground.

He doubled the spread as he
Followed his route.
He was the sole reason
The neighbors moved out.

But when it came roundup
This ranny was cheered
The doggondest wrangler
That ever was reared.

He brought in more cows than
A crew all combined
And burned his brand deeply
On every behind.

He needed no rope, for
This man of renown
Just blew out his breath and
The critters fell down.

Now this is a story of
Man at his best,
And why the wild garlic's
All gone from the West . . .

He broke off. "Pretty silly, isn't it?"
The girl was laughing, laughing so hard

that tears showed in the corners of her eyes. "Shamus, you're priceless."

"Well now —"

"Who would think a big, fighting man like you would make up anything like that?"

"Well, it's not much, and besides, I'm not a fighting man and you know it."

"I think you are," she said. "The greatest." She came into the bunkhouse and before he knew what she intended she reached up to clasp small hands at the back of his neck, pull his head down and kiss him fully on the mouth.

6

Belmont appeared quiet when Shamus Magee brought his horse into the main street and rode down to the livery. Not that he had expected much else; the town was usually quiet except on Saturday night.

He left his horse with the night hostler and started back up the sidewalk, headed for the Belmont Bar. Suddenly a shadow materialized from the building next to the livery. The shadow blocked his path.

There she stood, hands on hips, red hair flying loosely in the wind, not saying anything. Shamus stopped. He sidestepped and Marty Clare sidestepped with him. He took a step the other way and she followed the maneuver. He gave up.

"Look, Marty, it's after nine o'clock. You should be in bed. Does your father know you're out?"

"My father," she said, mimicking his tone, "is on an errand of mercy and doesn't give a damn where I am."

"You know that isn't true. Your father is a fine man."

"Who's arguing?"

"You're the darndest kid I ever saw. Why don't you leave me alone?"

"Because someone has to look after you. You haven't got sense enough to look after yourself."

Shamus tried to hold his temper. He found that it was not nearly as easy as it had been a week ago. "I'm perfectly able to take care of myself," he said fiercely. "How did you know I'd be in tonight anyway?"

"The whole town knows."

He stared at her. "What do you mean? How can they?"

"Burton sent three men in. They got here at five o'clock. By six everyone knew that you've declared war on the Bar X, that you were coming in to hire a crew, and that Burton had passed the word that anyone riding for you was liable to be in deep trouble."

Shamus whistled silently. This was coming a little fast. Not that he doubted her words. He knew how news could travel in Belmont.

"You haven't got the sense God gave a porcupine." She sounded disgusted. "Honest, Shamus, I'm just about ready to give up on you."

He groaned noisily, for effect, and because he really felt like groaning.

"What have I done now?"

"What haven't you done? I absolutely never saw anyone who could make such a complete fool of himself in twenty-four hours — and all because of a woman who is no better than she should be."

"Now just a minute. Wasn't it you who was mad at me because I wouldn't fight Burton over that horse?"

"That's just it. You wouldn't fight for your horse, but just let that woman make soft eyes at you . . . ! You'd have had right on your side if you'd fought about the horse."

"And I suppose I haven't right on my side now."

Her lips curled, and in the light from the store window her eyes looked green, rather than grey.

"Opinions," she said, "differ on that."

He told her sharply, "As usual you're talking about something you don't understand.

71

If you knew what Burton tried to do to Myra Dedge you'd be singing a different tune."

"Would I now?"

"Yes you would. Why, what can you know about her? You probably never saw her in your life."

"Oh yes I have. You forget, Mr. Shamus Magee, that I get around this valley quite a lot more than you do. And I ride with my eyes open, which is more than you can claim half the time. I've seen your Myra Dodge. What's more I've talked to her, and watched her soft, lying face and those baby eyes she uses on the men. What did she do to make you fight — feel your muscles and tell you what a big, upstanding man you are to protect a helpless, frail woman?"

He stirred uncomfortably. "It wasn't like that at all. It was the way Burton picked on her. Why, he was holding her prisoner at his ranch, trying to force her to marry him, and when she escaped he sent Bud Cole and two men to drag her back like a slave."

"Ha!"

"It's true. They came right into the hotel last night. I had to lick all three."

"I heard about that too, you wonderful big strong man."

He grabbed her shoulders. He wanted to

72

shake her until her small teeth rattled. It was the second time he had ever touched her.

She stood there in his grasp, straight, yet graceful as a sapling. "Go ahead, hit me."

"Damn you for a brat!" He let her go. "Your father should have spanked hell out of you a long time ago."

She screwed up her face, mocking him. "Want to try?"

He would have thoroughly enjoyed it, but he passed up the opportunity. Instead he said, "I'm wasting time on you. That's the way it was. She told me all about it."

"I doubt that. Did she tell you that Burton bought the Diamond D from old man Dodge? Oh, I'm not saying that Burton didn't pressure the old buzzard. He practically stole it for two thousand dollars, and then he gave Dodge a day to get out of the country. So Dodge left. So two months later this girl showed up. She had a bill of sale, signed by her uncle."

"Well?"

"Burton just laughed at her. He said she'd been suckered by the old man. He even took her into his office and showed her his bill of sale."

"I don't believe any of this."

"Don't believe it, you chowder-head. But

this is the way it happened. She got all tearful then. She said she was a poor lone female, and she had spent all her money buying the ranch, and she didn't have anywhere to go, and could she stay there until she found a place to live. Well, Burton is a human, although some people will dispute it, and a male as well. He must have gone a little soft, looking at her eyes, so he let her stay. And do you know what she did?"

Shamus didn't. Shamus didn't believe one word of this.

"She stole Burton's bill of sale. That's what she did. Right out of his strong box." Marty broke off, chuckling as if she could no longer told her mirth. "It couldn't have happened to a meaner guy, the old goat. It's just the kind of trick he'd pull on someone else, and I'd be all for her if she hadn't tried to put her gluey fingers on you."

He said, "Who told you this nonsense?"

"Bud Cole."

It was Shamus' turn to snort. "I wouldn't believe Bud on a stack of Bibles."

She nodded. "You couldn't get Bud within a mile of a single Bible. Still, he told me the truth. I'll bet on that."

"I won't. This just doesn't make sense. If Claude Burton had that bill of sale he'd have filed it at the courthouse, you know that."

"Act your age. Since when has Burton done things the way other people do? He owns the cattlemen's association, and the sheriff and the county attorney and the recorder all owe their jobs to him. At least they couldn't have been elected if he'd opposed them. So he'd file a thing like that when he got around to it."

Shamus rubbed his chin. What she said about Burton was true, but he still had no intention of believing the rest of the story. "And I suppose he didn't try to get her to marry him? I suppose he didn't lock her up in that cabin behind the meadow?"

"Oh, he locked her up all right, but he didn't try to marry her. She tried to marry *him*. She knew a good thing when she saw one."

"I suppose Bud Cole told you this too?"

"That he did."

"You and Cole seem to be on mighty friendly terms."

"Just because you're stupid enough not to appreciate me," she said airily, "doesn't mean I haven't got friends."

"You be careful of Cole. He's a rattle-snake."

"Look who's calling names."

He was getting more annoyed by the minute. Maybe he ought to look up Doc Clare and have a little talk. Maybe Marty shouldn't wait until fall to go away to school. He tried hard to marshal his thoughts.

"You keep contradicting yourself," he said. "A minute ago you said Burton didn't want to marry her, yet you admit that he locked her up. If he didn't want to marry her why did he do that?"

"I'll tell you if you'll shut up. She stole the bill of sale and after she hid or destroyed it she went and told him. She suggested that they could get married and combine the ranches. Oh, she put on a big act. Cole was listening. She told Burton what a big, strong man he was, and how he needed a woman like her, and how together they could control the whole valley. And Burton laughed at her."

"I don't believe it."

"He told her he could buy her kind for two dollars in any town in the territory."

Shamus made a noise in his throat.

"And then he threw her out — told her to keep the Diamond D and starve to death because no one would work for her."

"If Cole told you that, he —"

"So she went up to Hawthorne and hired

half a dozen bush jumpers and started bringing back the Diamond D cattle from the lower range. Burton cornered them and gave them an hour to get out of the country. They hightailed, and she was furious."

"Go ahead," he invited with weary resignation. "Tell the rest of it."

"So she went loco. She grabbed a rifle and started shooting at Burton's men. She was a bad shot and one of them got a rope on her. Cole said she was like a wildcat, clawing and scratching. They didn't know what to do with her, so Burton locked her up until she would get some sense and agree to leave."

"That's all of it?"

"That's all of it."

"Marty, you don't actually believe this, do you?" His tone was patient, as if he were trying to explain something to a none too bright child. "You say you've seen her. Do you really think she would do these things?"

"She'd cut your throat and drink your blood if it would do her any good."

He laughed. He couldn't help it. "You know something? I'm beginning to suspect that you're a little jealous of her."

"You're darn right I am. She's unfair competition and I know it. And I don't want her ruining you along with the rest."

"All the rest of what?"

"You'll find out. I'll bet she's ruined men wherever she was. I'll bet she's killed some too."

"Go away."

She stared at him.

"You mean you're going ahead after all I've just told you? Why, you poor, dim-witted saddle tramp. You just haven't got sense enough to come in when it rains. Letting a woman like that twist you around her little finger. Why, even Claude Burton saw right through her."

"I'm not Claude Burton."

"I'll say you're not. And before he gets through with you you'll be nothing. You'll be hanging from a tree, that's where you'll be." She choked for an instant and fought for control. "Well, I don't care. Let them hang you, let them shoot you down, let them drag you from a horse. I give up. I should have known. Doc said you weren't worth the powder to blow you up, and Doc's a smart man even if he is my father."

She whirled around and vaulted the hitch-rail and raced away to lose herself in the darkness at the far side of the street.

Shamus let his breath out with a whoosh. As used as he was to Marty's sudden changes of mood, she could still startle him witless.

Then in spite of himself he grinned. He wasn't mad at her. She was just an inveterate little gossip. His anger sought out Cole and Burton. Burton must have instructed his foreman, and probably the rest of the crew, to spread the stories about Myra Dodge. Yes, that had to be it.

And how right Myra had been in not going to the sheriff last night. Had she done so it would have brought the whispers into the open and only made things worse.

He set his jaws tightly. Well, there was no need to be surprised at anything Claude Burton would do. The man's whole life since first coming into the valley had been one questionable transaction after another. Anybody ruthless enough to drive off homesteaders with helpless children would not hesitate to lie about a lady if it suited his purpose.

He made a mental resolve to ram the falsehoods down Burton's throat the next time they met. As for Cole, the man annoyed him more than ever. It was bad enough to have Cole spreading slurs about Myra, but when the snake chose to relay them through Marty Clare, that made it a lot worse.

Marty was still nothing but a kid. And with a man like Cole stopping to talk to her . . . Shamus did not like to think about it.

He started down the street toward the Belmont Bar, more determined than ever to carry the fight to Burton. They had asked for it. They had broken every rule of decency by which Shamus had unconsciously patterned his life. Within him a rage was rising, but it was a cold-headed rage, a studying rage.

He would not do anything on the spur of the moment. He would take his time and plan his campaign. You could not afford mistakes when you went up against anything as powerful as the Bar X.

He reached the door of the Belmont Bar and paused to look up and down the dark street, wondering if Marty was still watching him. He flipped open the batwing doors and stepped in. He stopped, every muscle in his big body pulling taut. Halfway across the crowded room, Bud Cole and two of Burton's riders stood with their elbows on the bar, looking at him.

"Come in," Cole said. "We've been waiting for you, Magee."

7

Shamus Magee had seen saloon fights. He had even seen men shot to death. But never before had he been the central figure in what might well wind up as a killing.

Curiously he knew no fear. His attitude was detached, almost that of a spectator, as if he stood to one side watching himself and Budlong Cole and his Bar X riders.

He had fleeting seconds in which to wonder if his father had felt thus when the necessity to kill faced him, and a sympathy for that father unexpectedly took root in him and grew. It had never occurred to him to question his mother's attitude or action, but now in this moment which seemed to stretch to eternity, he knew that the right had not all been on her side. Had his mother tried to comprehend, to help his father, the lives of the Magees might have been different.

It came as a blinding flash of understanding, and then he forgot it, for both instinct and sense told him that neither he nor Budlong Cole had much of a chance to walk out of this room alive.

He caught a glimpse of Sam Goth's worried face behind the bar, and knew that Sam would help him if he dared, despite the fact that the Bar X furnished Belmont and its businesses with the biggest payroll in this part of the country.

But Belmont was like any other town, and the people in it had their likes and dislikes, their fears and hates. There were men in this room who owed him many things, whom he had always counted among his friends; but now, in this second when the chips were down, they seemed as remote as any strangers. No one in his right mind would buy a piece of this fight. No one would step forward to stand at his side.

He was alone in a way that he had never been alone before, and there was no escape. He had to kill or be killed, or maybe both. He steeled himself for the effort, his eyes centering on Cole.

The foreman had not moved. He stood as he had stood when Shamus came through the door, one elbow on the bar, his flat hat shoved far back on his dark head, his narrow face twisted into a mocking smile that had no warmth or mirth.

"We began to think you wouldn't get here," Cole said.

Shamus took two slow steps, halting again. Something told him that Cole did not mean to be the first to reach for a gun. There must be a reason for this, and he decided that

Burton had so ordered it. Their game would be to toy with him, to goad him into making the first hostile move, and then because of their numbers and Cole's known speed, they would blast him out of existence, claiming afterward that they had no choice.

He smiled a little as if sharing a secret joke with himself. "I usually get where I'm going, Cole."

Budlong Cole had sensed the change in Magee. He had never paid much attention to him before, considering him just another drifting rider who had a certain knack with horses. But now he grew cautious, studying. Not that he had changed his mind about killing Magee, but he had no intention of being shot in the process.

He moved suddenly, taking one long step away from the bar. He fully expected the movement to spook Magee, to force him to draw, but Shamus' nerves were steadier than Cole had counted on.

Shamus stood fast, ready, and in the second which followed he understood Cole's plan.

Dutch had been on Cole's left. His right hand, hidden between Cole's back and the bar, already held his gun, free of the holster.

Had Shamus tried to draw, Dutch would have shot him before Magee's gun cleared leather, and since every eye in the room was on Shamus there would have been none to swear that Dutch hadn't started his draw after Shamus went for his gun.

The knowledge of the trickery filled Shamus with a bursting rage, but he held it as Dutch, set to trigger edge, swung up the heavy weapon before he realized that Shamus' hands had not moved.

He stood there pointing it at Shamus' belly, a foolish look spreading over his broad, sullen face as he grasped the fact that the trap had not worked.

And then Shamus laughed. It was not from mirth as much as from the need to ease the pressure building up inside of him.

"Put it away, Dutch, unless you want to hang."

Cole cut in, then. His mouth resembled a white scar as he spoke with bloodless lips flattened against his teeth. "Go ahead and draw, Magee."

"You first." Shamus had mastered his rage. He felt washed out, cold inside as if he had been purged with ice water. "When I kill you I want a dozen witnesses to tell the sheriff you started it."

"I don't need to be told," a new voice said. The doors behind Shamus had been spread open silently and a small man had come into the room. Shamus did not turn. He knew the voice.

"Come on in, Sheriff. With the audience we're getting maybe we should charge admission."

Luke Ronson did not answer. Instead he walked by Shamus and stopped before Bud Cole. Cole towered a head taller than the sheriff and was thirty pounds heavier.

"Clear out, Bud. That's all the trouble tonight."

Hot insolence flared in Cole's eyes. "This isn't your business, Luke. The man's a horse thief. Now he's trying to start a war."

"I know all about it," Ronson said. "Pull out, and tell Burton to keep his trouble out of this town."

"Are you telling Burton what to do, Luke? Aren't you forgetting something? Who pinned that tin badge to your vest?"

The sheriff did not change expression. He was past middle age, a wiry man with a thin face and greying hair. He had served the county for years, first as jailer, then as deputy and since the last election as sheriff. That he had won the election surprised no one. The old sheriff was retiring. Luke had never offended anyone during his years around the courthouse, and Burton and the

85

big ranchers to the south considered him safe.

They had small need for a law officer since they preferred to make their own version of the law. What they wanted was a man who would carry out the mechanics of the office without interfering in their affairs, and for this role Luke Ronson seemed just about perfect.

Therefore, not only Bud Cole but also Shamus Magee was surprised that Ronson would even come into the bar.

"I'll not tell you again, Bud." The sheriff's voice was steady. "Ride out, or I'll deputize every man in here and throw you in jail."

Cole hesitated. He knew the Bar X crew was not well liked in Belmont. These townsmen would hesitate to go against him on their own, but if called upon by the sheriff they would take pleasure in helping to lock him up.

Frustration made his voice hoarse. "What are you doing — changing sides? Throwing in with Magee?"

"I'm throwing in with no one," Ronson said. "I'm giving you one minute. Bud."

Cole made his decision. "Come on, boys. We'll catch Magee where his friends don't wear badges."

"Wait," Shamus said. "A message to Burton. Tell him to stop his lies — and stop yours — or I'll ride into the Bar X and make the both of you eat your words."

"Why you —" Cole started for him, but Ronson moved with amazing speed, stepping between them, jerking his gun free and shoving it into Bud's stomach. "That's enough, get out."

"He called me a liar!"

"Tell him you're sorry, Shamus."

"Hell with it. A man who lies about a woman is a dog."

Without taking his gaze off Cole the sheriff said in his new voice with the bite in it: "Give me your gun, Magee."

Shamus was startled. "What?"

"Your gun, damn it. Then go over to the rear table and sit down. If you open your mouth again I'll blow your fool head off."

For an instant Shamus hesitated. He was standing behind the sheriff. There was nothing Ronson could do if he refused. But he did not refuse. The little lawman was trying to halt the fight. He admired Ronson for trying, even if he wasn't sure in his own mind that he wanted the fight halted.

Slowly he reached down and lifted the heavy weapon. The sheriff put his left hand behind his back and Shamus reversed the gun and put the grip in his palm. Then he ambled toward the rear of the room.

He knew he had called Cole at the wrong moment, but damn it, the man had to stop lying about Myra. He turned and sat down. Luke Ronson had the three Bar X men in front of him, herding them to the door. They disappeared and then he heard the half muffled sound of running hoofs as they tore up the street and out of town. As the last sound faded into the night, Ronson came back into the room.

The stiffness had deserted his body and he looked tired and small and without significance. The air of command was gone, completely gone. He walked over to Shamus and shook his head and clucked and handed him his gun.

"Magee, what's got into you? You were one rider who minded his own business and kept out of foolish trouble. Now you're trying to act like a two-bit gunman."

Shamus stood up. He could usually talk better standing up. "Luke, I thank you for the accident that brought you in here tonight, but don't push me."

"It was no accident," Ronson said. "Doc Clare's kid came busting into my office and said the Bar X was murdering you."

Shamus' mouth fell open. Marty had said she was through with him, but she still

88

couldn't keep her small nose out of things. She had tried to help him, mad as she was. The thought brought a warm, pleasant sensation.

"The same thing I told Cole applies to you," Ronson said. "Don't start trouble, Shamus. I mean it."

"I didn't start this and you know it. Who turned my horses out of the livery corral?"

Luke Ronson did not pretend to misunderstand. "You could have come to the courthouse and sworn out a warrant."

"What good would that have done?"

Luke Ronson was an honest man, honest enough to be aware of his own weakness. He was by habit a job-holder, content to work at routine chores, avoiding trouble when possible, and he realized that he had taken action tonight only because of a driving fear that this trouble might spread into a full sized conflict.

He said, "Let's try and be reasonable, Shamus."

"Sure," Shamus said. "Let's be reasonable. A lot of people have tried to reason with Claude Burton. They had their homes burned, their wives and children turned out. Some of them left the country. Others pulled back into the mountains around Hawthorn where they freeze and starve and live on what they can steal. Sure, let's be reasonable."

He did not realize that he had been making a speech until he glanced around and saw that everyone in the room was watching, listening intently. He flushed, but stubbornness drove him on.

"We want to be reasonable too, but when Burton locks up my boss in a cabin and then spreads all kinds of stories about her, it's a little difficult. I don't want any trouble with you or with anyone else in the valley, but I'm serving warning right now. We're not going to back down. We're going to keep the cows the Diamond D owns, and the grass we own, and we're going to keep Burton off of us. Does that make sense, or am I supposed to go around tipping my hat every time Bud Cole speaks?"

Ronson wet his lips. "I — well, I don't know what to say."

"Don't say anything. Just remember, if trouble starts we didn't start it. Now, I came in to hire a crew, and nobody, not even you, has the right to stop me."

Luke Ronson signed. The trouble he dreaded was here. Burton would never back down on anything, and it looked as if Magee could be just as mulish.

"Just don't do anything to make me come

after you," he said, and knew it sounded weak to every man who heard it. Somehow, somewhere, he had lost the fine edge of authority he had held before Cole left. Suddenly he wanted to be out of that room.

He turned away, moving toward the door, conscious of the silence behind him. When the batwings flapped behind him, Shamus Magee gave his attention to the rest of the room. He walked to the bar and said:

"Set up the house."

It was not the first time Shamus had ordered drinks for everyone in this same bar. He was by nature a sociable man, and when he had money he never hesitated to spend it.

But now there was a difference. He was working for a ranch, trying to hire men. He noticed, without appearing to, a certain reluctance in accepting his invitation, and he frowned a little to himself.

He knew just about everybody here. Half of these fellows were townsmen, working in the stores and shops of Belmont. The rest were idle hands, laid off after the spring branding, waiting for haying season and then the fall roundups. From the latter group he hoped to recruit his crew. He watched them anxiously as they came to the bar. He waited until the drinks were poured, until he had emptied his own glass. Then he turned, resting both elbows on the bar, his back against its rounded edge.

"I need ten men. I'll pay fifty and found and a bonus to every man who stays through roundup."

There was a murmur of surprise. The pay was good, ten dollars above what top hands were getting at the big outfits. Shamus watched their faces, trying to guess what went on in their minds. He knew Cole had warned everyone not to work for him, but the cowboy is by nature a stubborn, independent animal who hates to be pushed, or told what he cannot do.

Yet no one moved, no one came forward to accept. Shamus had never hired men before. He did not know quite how to go about it.

He did not make the mistake of thinking they were cowards. These men in their way were brave enough; they simply were not gunfighters or toughs. Had they already been on the Diamond D payroll they would have fought, for no one in the world is more loyal to his salt than a cowboy. But they felt no loyalty to Myra Dodge and they hesitated to step into a fight which could very easily be lost and lost fast.

He wanted to jeer at them, to ask if they

feared Burton to the point that they would not take a job without his consent. But he did not. Some inner instinct warned him that jeers would not work. And he certainly could not afford the luxury of making more enemies than he already had.

He watched them mutter some excuse and turn away, and the anger which had lain dormant in him for the last few minutes began to rise again.

He turned around, ignoring their muttered excuses, and stared solidly at the back-bar mirror, knowing that he had failed. The scrape of feet behind him ceased, and the door made its squeaking swing for the last time, and he said bitterly, "You should sue me for running off your trade, Sam."

Sam Goth pretended unconcern as he gathered up the dirty glasses. "What did you expect, Shamus?"

"Too much," Shamus said. "I thought there might be one man, two men, maybe half a dozen who are a little tired of Burton playing God."

"They're tired of him."

"Then why in hell won't they join up and fight?"

Goth stopped mopping the bar. "Would you have joined if one if one of them had come to you two weeks ago? And yet Burton hasn't changed. He's been acting the same way since I've known him."

Shamus wet his finger in a puddle of spilled liquor and drew a pattern on the bar. "Yeah, sure, but —"

"But you hadn't met that woman then," Sam said, "and you hadn't listened to her."

"Let's keep her out of it."

"Sure," Goth said. "Keep her out. I wish you'd never seen her, boy. You've changed. I watched when you came in here tonight. You were ready to shoot it out. You were almost eager to kill."

"Look," Shamus said. "I learned something tonight. I've told you about my father, and my mother, and how I always figured the old man was wrong, and tried consciously not to be like him."

Goth watched him, saying nothing.

Shamus passed a hand across his face. "I'm a little mixed up, Sam. I'm not sure now that Ma was right. Maybe if she had stuck it out things would have been different with him, and I'd have had a chance to know him. Sometimes it seems that a man can get into a spot where he has to fight, not only to keep alive but to be able to live with himself. Maybe those men had to be killed. Maybe my father was right, as I'm right tonight. Who knows? You don't, I don't."

"I guess so." Goth was cautious.

"So Burton thinks he's beaten me, all he has to do is send his lying foreman around to pass the word that we're poison, and he's won. He's used that way before. It's worked fine up to now. There's hardly a spread left north of Belmont except his. Well, I haven't been licked and I don't scare, and the girl I work for doesn't scare either. We'll hold the Diamond D and if he tries to throw us off he's the one who will get hurt."

"Without a crew?"

Magee poured a second drink. "I'll get a crew."

"Where?"

"Up at Hawthorn."

They stared at each other.

"There are plenty in those hills who hate Burton, and rightly so. I'll give them a chance to fight, to fight together, not to get picked off singly as they were before. Then we'll see how Burton likes being hazed the way he's hazed people all his life."

"You'll turn the ranchers south against you."

Magee exploded. "Turn them against me? Aren't they already against me? Did one of them ever protest anything Burton chose to do? Don't give me that. The minute a man gets three thousand cows he's Mister Big, and ordinary people can freeze and starve as long as they keep out of his way."

A low laugh came from a rear corner of the room. Shamus swung around, startled. He had thought they were entirely alone. He could not see the spot in the mirror because the angle was wrong.

Tim Younger sat at the corner table, holding a deck of battered cards in his slim hands. He riffled them absently. "Keep talking," he said. "I love it."

Shamus turned and walked toward him, not knowing whether to be angry or not.

"What are you doing here?"

"Listening." Younger's lean, sun-darkened face split in a mocking grin. "Maybe you should run for Congress, or do you mean it?"

"I mean it."

Younger dropped the cards so that they scattered across the cloth table top. He stood up, hitching his gunbelt around as he did so. "All right, what are we waiting for? Let's go."

Shamus scowled at him. "Meaning what?"

"Hiring men, aren't you?"

"That's right."

"You've hired one."

Shamus considered him and there was no softening in his face. "Just why do you want to work for me?"

Younger yawned. "Maybe the purse is thin. Maybe I don't like using a hay fork. Or maybe I just don't like Burton."

Shamus hesitated for only a moment. "All right, get the horses."

Younger nodded. The rear door was closer and he used it. Shamus went back to the bar to pay for the drinks. Goth shook his head.

"Shamus, you're making a mistake."

"How? Fighting Burton? You trying to defend Burton?"

"Of coures I'm not." Goth was nettled. "You're hiring a crew because they hate Burton. Don't you realize that?"

"I do."

"And Younger. He's no good."

"He's tough. No one ever walked on him."

"No one ever walked on a rattlesnake either, but I wouldn't want to take one to bed with me."

Shamus tossed money on the bar. He turned without speaking and went out into the dark street.

8

Shamus Magee studied Tim Younger as they rode through the night. He had never known Younger very well, and never liked much what he did know about him.

But he had to admit that Younger probably suited his purpose better than anyone else who had been in the bar. Not that he hunted trouble or made a nuisance of himself. It was just that he held his own counsel, and discouraged overtures from the more gregarious people of the town, and was genuinely a tough hombre.

He had drifted in two or three years ago and taken a job with the stage line. Twice there had been attempted holdups, and twice Younger had killed the would-be bandit. Then he had quit to guide a party of engineers who were investigating the possibility of running a grade for a railroad through the mountains to the west. The grade had been found too costly and the line shifted some seventy miles farther north.

Since then Younger had hung around Belmont, taking a few odd riding jobs, but spending most of his time gambling. Now and then he disappeared, only to turn up again without a word to explain his absence.

Younger was not a talkative man and they covered better than five miles in silence before the rifle cut its sharp, whip-like sound out of the darkness. Younger had been slightly in front, and the ball caught his horse in the neck and knocked the animal out from under him.

He fell spread-eagled, arms wide, legs wide, as if searching for support which was not there.

Shamus reacted without thinking, twisting his horse around to charge the clump of bushes from which the shot had come, firing as he rode in.

The rifle exploded almost in his face. The shot made an angry whistle as it tore past his head. He ducked instinctively, even as he saw the bushwhacker leap up and try to run.

He killed the man automatically, without thought, without aiming, and leaped out of the saddle, thinking that the attacker was probably not alone.

But nothing moved in the brush, and no sound came as he crouched there, studying the ground around him. Slowly, carefully he moved over to where the attacker lay and turned him so that he could see the solid face in the thin moonlight. It was the Bar X rider, Dutch.

He straightened, cursing under his breath. They had ridden the road without thought of ambush, but now he knew that from here on out he would never be safe, anywhere, day or night. He had a lot to learn about the game as played under Claude Burton's rules. Another thoughtless move, another lapse of caution and he would be dead.

It was the first time he had killed a man, but he felt no guilt, no real regret. Dutch had waited there in the darkness to kill him. There were no rules, actually. Only success or failure counted in this heartless game. Dutch had failed, and paid for that failure with his life.

He turned away, and caught his horse, and led it back to the trail where Younger was picking himself up gingerly from rutted ground.

"You hurt?"

Younger shook himself as if to see that all his bones were still in place. "Guess not. How many were there?"

"One."

"We should have watched for it." Younger walked stiffly to his fallen horse and took one brief look at the animal. He did not ask Shamus if he had killed the man. He knew. "Did he have a horse?"

"I suppose so."

"We'd better find it. Mine isn't worth a damn." He bent to loosen his saddle from the dead animal. Shamus went back, searching for the other horse.

He found it in a draw a good two hundred feet from the road and led it to where Younger waited beside his saddle. Younger pulled off Dutch's saddle and replaced it with his own. He seemed completely unmoved by his near brush with death, coolly unaffected by the fact that Dutch lay dead only a few feet away.

"We'd better bury him," Shamus said.

"Why?" Younger glanced around. "You think he'd have bothered to bury me if he'd been a better shot?"

Shamus guessed not.

"Let the Bar X do it," Younger said. "When he doesn't show up by morning they'll come out looking." He swung up into the saddle.

Callousness like that offended Shamus. Death, he realized, meant nothing to Tim Younger, and as he mounted and dropped in beside the man he speculated about him. Somewhere Younger had been case hardened, somewhere he had ridden outside the law. That much was obvious. The way he held himself, always on guard, the watchful way his eyes shifted before he entered a strange room, his mockery of danger, and his utter failure to react to the basic emotions which governed most men.

Why, then, had he elected to work for the Diamond D? Certainly not for the extra high wages Magee had offered. If he stayed through roundup he would gain only a few dollars above what he could have drawn from another outfit.

It had to be one of two things. Either he hated Burton so thoroughly that he was willing to throw in with what looked like a lost cause for a chance to attack the rancher, or he had some reason of his own which did not appear on the surface.

Almost automatically Magee ruled out the first possibility. If Younger hated Burton so deeply, all he had to do was wait for opportunity to bushwhack the man and then ride out of the country. No, there had to be a better reason. Certainly he wasn't moved by any sympathy for Myra Dodge. A man like Younger just didn't care. Lies about Myra would not arouse his anger. More likely they would tickle his cynical humor. Shamus decided that he had better watch Younger. He sighed. He would have to watch Mushy Calder too.

It was not enough that he had Burton to worry about. He must worry about the men he was hiring to help him. He glanced ahead. Already the sky to the east showed a streak of crimson. Soon the sun would rise over the hills to drive away the lingering shadows.

But it was still only half light when they reached the Diamond D lane and turned into it. A lamp burned in the main house as they tramped into the yard.

Mushy Calder stepped from the bunkhouse doorway, carrying a rifle, yawning as he came. His eyes flicked when he recognized Tim Younger but he made no comment. The girl came hurrying down the path from the house.

"Any luck?"

Shamus had been dreading this moment. He jerked his head toward Younger and said, "This is Tim Younger. No one else would come. Burton's men had spread the word."

He saw the disappointment wash across her face, but not hopelessness. She was not a person who ever gave up. "But you said —"

He knew what he had said. He had been so certain that his friends would rally to his aid. Actually, he thought, if it had been for his personal help some of the men might have taken the offer. But not for a stranger, even a woman.

He said, "We aren't through. I said I'd get a crew and I will."

"Where?"

He sensed that both Calder and Younger were standing behind him, listening, watching. "Hawthorn."

"You objected to that before," she said. "You told me the people up there were outlaws, that if we tried to hire them it would turn the southern ranchers against us."

"I know I did." He had the feeling that he was being driven. "But now we have no choice, not unless you want to ride out of the valley, not unless you want to quit without a fight."

"You know I don't." She had stepped up close to him, so that she could place one slim hand on his arm, so that she could look up into his face.

Her nearness made his voice a little unsteady. "All right. Don't worry about it. Let me get a couple of hours sleep and I'll ride up and see what can be done."

"You haven't eaten?"

He shook his head.

"I'll get something. I'll have it in ten minutes." She moved quickly toward the house. He uncinched his saddle and turned the horse into the corral. When he came back from the gate he saw Younger watching him, and he knew a sudden unreasonable desire to slap the smirk from the knowing face.

9

Two hours before noon, Shamus and Tim Younger walked their horses out of the ranch lane and took the road north. Shamus had not actually wanted Younger's company, but something in the way the man looked at Myra Dodge made him uneasy, and at the last moment he had decided to bring him along.

Mushy Calder remained at the ranch. Shamus had ordered him to keep two horses saddled, and at the first sign of attack from the Bar X, to take the girl and ride north.

The valley at this point narrowed until the two mountain ranges were less than four miles apart, and the flat lands around Belmont gave way to rolling country which rose gradually to meet the timbered slopes of the foothills.

To the north, the mountains closed together at the valley's upper end, a wild country of narrow canyons and rising rocky peaks. This Diamond D range was not as good as that farther south in the waist of the valley, and at first thought it seemed that Claude Burton was being foolish in attempting to claim it. But Shamus knew that Burton never did anything foolish where business was concerned. A good, solid, definite reason lay behind his effort to annex this ranch.

As long as a foreign outfit held this grass he had a long, hard-to-maintain line fence to worry him. If this were all Bar X land his cattle could range at will, clear to the timbered slopes, for the country above was so rugged that few if any cattle would stray into the hills.

That the people around Hawthorn rustled some stock was an open secret, but there was no road beyond Hawthorn, no trail over which cattle could be hazed in any number. The mountains here were so rugged that they made a natural fence and the few cows stolen were taken to be eaten rather than to be sold.

They rode steadily, silently. Ahead of them the mountains lifted abruptly, seeming to offer a wall that could not be pierced. On the right, beside the rushing stream, the jumble of the old smelter rose from the covering brush, its metal roofs broken and rusting, its two chimneys pointing like ghostly fingers toward the cloudless sky.

Here ore had been brought in wagons from the mine above. The waste piles made small mountains beside the stream, the ruts which had been cut in the rocky soil by the iron wagon wheels still showing plainly despite the lapse of time.

The mine had been worked in the late sixties and early seventies, but a good ten years had passed since the last fire had been built in the smelter, the last yellow smoke had poured from its stacks.

Beyond the buildings the trail made a sharp turn to the right, and plunged almost at once into the canyon which the Belmont River had dug through the tough country rock. It was a narrow cleft, twisting and winding up from the high valley floor, climbing over three thousand feet before it reached the mining town above.

Shamus never rode the trail without marveling anew at the labor and ingenuity men would expend in their search for wealth. At times the canyon was hardly wider than the rushing river which had given it its birth. Here the miners had by hand toil cut a shelf from the rock wall itself, a shelf wide enough to accomodate the heavy ore wagons and their teams of struggling mules.

Up this cleft Younger rode ahead, the chop

of their horses' hoofs drowned by the splashing tumult of the rushing stream. They rode slowly but steadily, looping back upon themselves as the road climbed until it seemed that they must reach the summit of the range.

But as they came into the lower end of the semi-deserted town the peaks still loomed ahead and above them, showing white and glistening in the late afternoon sun.

Above the town and the shattered buildings of the mine the main canyon boxed out, ending abruptly in a sheer face of rock which rose nearly a thousand feet to the reaching peaks.

The town itself sprawled untidily in a kind of bowl, with side canyons running back toward the west like probing fingers. To the east and north the buildings of the mine and the entrances to the haulage tunnels marred the mountainside.

Timber had sprouted along the old ore chutes and on the breasts of the old dumps, partly masking the marks man had made as he tore at the entrails of the mountain.

The mine buildings were near collapse. The heavy winter snows had sagged their roofs and twisted the supporting timbers so that they stood on the steep slope like drunken giants, ready to pitch headlong into the town below.

Hawthorn had boasted a dozen streets, criscrossing each other across the bowl, with houses climbing up the sides and perching along the stretches of side canyons.

Once this town had held thirty-five hundred people, working in the mine, serving in the stores, the dancehalls and the saloons which furnished the miners' entertainment. Now fewer than a hundred people lived in the place, some of them refugees driven from the valley below by Burton's ruthless hounding, others wanted men who had found in Hawthorn a certain security with the law far away.

What they lived on was a mystery in itself. Some undoubtedly stole a few cows now and then, others worked sporadically at hi-grading the old dumps or searching for neglected pockets in the deserted mine drifts which honey-combed the rock face above.

Shamus had never given it much thought before. He knew Hawthorn and liked it. The place had an air of decay but it was restful, and he had hunted up the side canyons and through the timbered slopes to the west of town.

He pulled up before the only store still

open and stepped down, waiting for Younger to join him. Then they mounted to the porch and crossed it to come into the big room.

Originally the building had been the town's largest saloon, the room a good hundred feet in depth with a width half that amount. The back bar, rich with crystal mirrors, still stood against the side wall, and the ornamental lamps still hung from the high ceiling, but the place was now stacked with goods of all kinds, the aisles so narrow between the counters and tables that it was difficult to make your way.

The goods displayed were a curious mixture, staples which the mountain people could not live without, mingled with the salvage gleaned from the abandoned stores and shops up and down the crooked streets.

The man who presided at this bazaar-like mess was as curious as any of the goods his sagging counters displayed. Ed Crowley was not old as years went, but he lived his life in the past. He gave his real interest not to the happenings of today, but to things that had happened in the town twenty years ago.

He came forward now, large and fat, his black beard hiding the whole lower half of his heavy-jowled face, and there was no welcome in his manner. His voice was brusque, almost unfriendly.

"What are you doing here, Shamus?"

Shamus Magee blinked at him. He had always gotten on well with Crowley and the rest of the people in the mountain town. Mostly they resented strangers, being suspicious of their motives for being there.

But Shamus had been considered almost one of their own. He had not been identified with any of the big ranchers whom they hated, nor was he a stock detective or law officer.

He said, "Golly, Ed, what have I done now?"

Crowley planted himself before them. He glanced at Younger and a subtle change in his expression hinted that he recognized the man and was surprised to find him with Magee.

"It's not what you've done," he said in his grumbling voice. "It's what you're going to do. You're up here to hire men."

Shamus started. He had not been surprised that the news of his hiring had preceded him to Belmont last night, but he was surprised that the news had reached Hawthorn. There was very little communication between the two towns.

"Who told you that?"

"One of Burton's men. He came up here

last night, and he made it very plain. He said that if anyone from here dared to sign with you Burton would bring up his full crew and hunt out every man in the hills and hang them. And burn this store, too, by God. Burn this town."

His voice broke a little on the last word as if he could not stand to contemplate the thought. "This town, my town."

Younger said cynically, "That might be a good idea — burn it before it falls apart."

In an undertone Shamus Magee told him to shut up. There was no need to antagonize Crowley more than need be. The storekeeper was a kind of unofficial mayor of the place and he had ways of bringing men to heel when he wanted to. If Crowley opposed them it might be difficult to hire men.

His tone was still easy as he said, "Who's running Hawthorn, Ed, you or Burton?"

The stream of profanity which poured from Crowley's lips left no doubt about his feeling for Burton. "I'd like to see him blasted from the earth," he said after he paused for breath, "but what can we do?"

"You can fight," Shamus told him. "If you'd all stick together you could fight. Burton never had more than twenty men working for him at any time. You must have fifty or more, hidden in the brush."

The big man wiped his bearded lips with the back of a fat, none too clean hand. "You don't understand. He wouldn't come alone. He's too clever for that. He'd swear we were outlaws. He'd get help from the southern ranchers. He might even bring the sheriff to make it look legal."

"The sheriff wouldn't stand for him burning the town," Shamus said.

"Wouldn't he? Has the sheriff or anyone ever stopped Burton from what he wanted to do? The man is a devil, and only a fool fights the devil. My father started this store, and twenty years ago it was the biggest between Denver and Salt Lake City. You can ask anyone."

Shamus just waited, watching him.

"This town was wonderful then, wonderful, and it will be again. Why, you should have seen it on Saturday nights, twenty-one saloons, three dance halls, and the girls, you never saw such girls."

His eyes seemed to burn with the memory, and it came to Shamus that Crowley was not quite sane.

He said softly, "Mines play out, Ed, and things change."

"This mine never played out." Crowley's voice grated belligerently. "There's just as much gold and silver and copper in that ridge as there ever was. My father knew it, and I know it. That's why we stayed when the other fools moved out."

"Then why did they close the mine?"

"It was the vultures that did it, the stock-brokers. They didn't care about the mine, or the town or the ore. They were like Burton, always tearing down what better men had built."

Younger made a cynical noise with his lips but Shamus nudged his arm. Crowley did not notice. He was too engrossed in his own words to notice anything. His voice had gained the fanatical note of a revivalist.

"I remember when they came here to talk to old man Timmons, them in their broadcloth clothes and iron hats, wearing more diamonds than a Cripple Creek gambler. They told lies all through the country. They offered Timmons a million dollars for the mine, and he took it. Signed the papers right in this self-same room. Then they reincorporated and took the smelter reports east, and they sold seven million shares of stock. Seven million. And did the money go to running the mine? It did not. They bled the place white, taking only the easy-to-reach reserves which Timmons had blocked out. After that they stole every cent from the treasury and there was no money to operate. They tried to assess the stockholders for more, and when they failed, the mine closed down."

He went over and sat on an upended nail keg as if his legs would no longer support his heavy body. He buried his bearded face in his hands and with a shock Shamus realized that the man was crying.

He said gently, "I heard another story, Ed. I heard that there was too much water, that the mine flooded."

The words arrested Crowley's grief. "Flooded? Here, let me show you." He went around the long bar and pulled open a drawer in the back bar, bringing forth a long roll of paper which Shamus thought was a map.

When Crowley unrolled it he saw his mistake. It was a chart showing the shafts, the tunnels and the drifts of the mine.

"Look at this." Crowley's finger was slightly unsteady as he indicated a line at the bottom of the page. "Know what that is? I'll tell you. It's a drainage tunnel, over a mile long. They drove it clear through the ridge to come out in Pine Valley on the far side of the mountain. It drained all the upper workings, and they cut ore chutes inside the hill so they could drop their ore into the tunnel and haul it out. They even planned another smelter at the Pine Valley end so they wouldn't have to haul down the Belmont grade."

Shamus stared at the plat. Younger said in a bored voice, "Are we going mining, or do we hire some men?"

Crowley looked up as if he had forgotten the reason they were in Hawthorn. He stood still for a moment, the fire dying from his eyes; then slowly, almost lovingly he rolled up the chart and placed it carefully in the drawer.

Shamus was not impressed by Crowley's belief in the old mine. Every abandoned mining camp in the country had at least one man who refused to give up hope, refused to believe that the veins which had produced so much riches had at last played out.

He said slowly, "Can you still get through the tunnel into Pine Valley?"

Crowley shook his head. "It's blocked. The old boards holding one of the ore chutes gave way a couple of years ago and dumped a thousand tons of rock into that tunnel." He came around the end of the bar and his voice changed again. "But it will be opened some day, and this town will grow again, and when it does, I'll be here. I own most of the buildings that are left. Now do you see why I can't let Burton burn the place, why I can't let anyone living here do something which might make Burton mad?"

Shamus could understand, but he also had his own problem. He said, "You're looking at it wrong, Ed. Two or three times in the last couple of years Burton's ridden into the hills and picked off a couple of men for rustling."

Crowley shrugged heavily.

"There will always be some rustling as long as these people live up here," Shamus continued. "Now supposing Burton succeeds in running us out of the Diamond D. That means his stock will graze clear up into the hills. The more animals that get into the timber, the more are going to be killed. Sooner or later Burton will decide that Hawthorn has to go. Am I right?"

The misery in Crowley's eyes told him that the fat man agreed.

"Your people won't be strong enough to fight him alone, and they won't be organized," Shamus said. "They'll just fade back into the mountains as they've done before, and you'll be left to try and defend your town alone."

He knew that his arguments were going home.

"So let me hire them, organize them, Crowley. Then we can fight together with a chance of winning. You talk to them. They might not listen to me, but they will listen to you. If we can hold the Diamond D, its range will serve as a kind of buffer zone between you and Burton — and I'll guarantee that as long as I'm there, no one in these hills is going to starve for want of a little meat. You know me, Crowley. I won't forget my friends."

Crowley nodded slowly. "Let me think. Give me a couple of hours to talk with some of them. Maybe you're right. Maybe the time has come to fight."

10

"You know something?" Tim Younger said. "I was joking last night, but maybe you should run for Congress. You sure make pretty speeches."

Shamus reddened, embarrassed. "I wasn't trying to, but we need men, and if Ed Crowley is against us we haven't got much chance."

"Think you won him over?"

Shamus rubbed his puffed cheek reflectively. "I'd say maybe yes. Crowley hates Burton, and he's afraid of him, and he knows that sooner or later Burton is going to ride up here and wipe this place off the map. If that happened it would kill him. It's all he's got, the store and that town."

Younger glanced up and down the windy street. "The old coot is crazy."

"I suppose he is."

"You know that mine's worked out?"

"I guess so."

Younger snickered. "Or maybe you think there's gold just waiting for someone to dig out?"

Shamus had never thought much about it before. "Think I'll climb up and have a look around. We can't hurry Crowley. It will take him the rest of the afternoon to talk to a few people and make up his mind. If we push him, he'll just get stubborn. Want to come along?"

"For what?" Younger yawned. "I never did like climbing."

Shamus hesitated. Actually he did not care much for the idea himself, but something in Crowley's words had awakened his curiosity. He saw Younger seat himself on the top porch step, his back against a post, and pull his hat down to shield his eyes from the slanting sun.

"All right. See you later." The street he traveled had been the town's main thoroughfare. He kept to its center because the old board walks which ran in front of the deserted stores were rotten and unsafe. As he moved forward he tried to picture the way the street had looked in its heyday, and failed. It was almost impossible to conjur a vision of the town with people thronging its sidewalks, with wagons and buckboards and buggies cramming its roadways.

He passed the hotel, two-storied and pretentious, its sign still legible, tattered curtains still hanging in long shreds at the glassless windows. Part of the metal roof had blown into the street below and no one had troubled to remove the twisted metal. Another five years of wind and snow and rain and there would be little left. The mine buildings stood at the head of the street, close under the rock face which blocked the canyon's upper end. To his right, a thousand feet away, the Belmont River dropped over the face, falling, twisting, tumbling down a six hundred foot drop to rush away into the valley below.

It was not a pretty stream, nor a continuous fall, for in places the water ran through rock caves and was lost to sight. In others it poured over boulders and logs, caught in the upthrust of jagged stone which rose from the mountainside like so many hungry teeth.

He climbed the dump and walked through

the rising tiers of sheds which housed the crushing machinery. Most of this was gone, carted away so that its stamps could pound out the ore of some other mine. But the shafts and donkey engines still remained, and the huge drum with its rusting, broken cable which had been used to haul the loaded ore cars from the slanting tunnel.

He stood looking around him at the desolation, viewing the wreckage of man's hopes. Although he had been in the town many times before he had never before had interest enough to prompt him to enter the mine buildings.

Through a hole in the roof he could see the headframe and bull wheel of one of the shafts high on the slope above him. They had attacked the ridge from a dozen different places, sinking shafts from the summit, driving drifts along splintered veins, honeycombing the mountain in their quest, for the whole area was highly mineralized and the veins fractured and faulted by some long forgotten volcanic action.

But it was the drainage tunnel which interested him. It opened directly behind the abandoned mill, pitching into the hill on a long, inclined slant. He judged that this had been done to force drainage the other way and because future plans had called for a new smelter at the Pine Valley end.

Why had the engineers chosen to do this rather than continue to use the smelter beside the Belmont? He could only guess. Maybe they had run out of wood for charcoal on this side. The mine had been a hungry giant, denuding the slopes of their huge trees until little was left except the second growth pole pine and aspen.

He stared at the tunnel's dark, square mouth with its crossed timber face, holding the mountainside above it, and wished suddenly that he had a lamp. He had never before had any real desire to go underground, but now he wanted to see for himself the mine which had evoked such enthusiasm from Ed Crowley.

And then he caught a flicker of light far down the dark passage. At first he thought his eyes were playing tricks on him, but as he watched it came again, and then he heard the clink of metal on rock.

Somebody was coming out of the tunnel!

The fact startled him. Everything had been so quiet, with a stillness which is associated with death. Then he laughed.

There was no real reason to be surprised. He had known for a long time that there were snipers in the mine, men crawling through the deserted drifts looking for pockets of high-grade, for quartz stringers which had been neglected by the original miners.

One of these men was coming out. Maybe he could borrow the lamp and creep back for a look himself.

He waited, standing a little to one side, not thinking of concealment, but rather that he ought not to startle the miner until he was clear of the tunnel.

The miner was a woman. Shamus could not have been more amazed if a ghost had walked out into the engine house. Particularly because the woman was Marty Clare.

She stopped just inside the tunnel entrance, looking around as if she did not quite know where she was. Then she saw him, and dropped the small, double-bitted miner's pick she had been carrying.

"Shamus!"

He moved toward her. "What are you doing here?"

She stooped to retrieve the pick. Her red hair was tucked up under the miner's cap and a carbide lamp sent its tiny open flame into the still, stale air.

She had a moment of grace before she straightened. "I might ask you that," she said tartly, "but I think I can guess."

He said, "That doesn't answer my question. I certainly didn't expect you to pop from the earth. What in the world are you doing in the old mine?"

She walked by him to peer through a hole in the plank wall where a board had fallen away, as if to assure herself of where she really was. Then she turned and said a trifle sharply, "Why shouldn't I be here? I like to explore the mine. Ask me some day and I'll show you some of the ore I've picked up."

He told himself that he shouldn't have been surprised. She had roamed the country far and wide, much more than he had, and she did not know the meaning of fear.

"You shouldn't do it," he told her sternly. "That can be dangerous. Only a fool goes underground alone." He had heard miners say that somewhere. "What if you got trapped? What if some of the rotting timbers gave way? Does your father know about this?"

Suddenly her grey green eyes flecked frantically. "You won't tell him. Please, Shamus, you can't tell him."

He had never seen Marty Clare show real fear before. "Why not?" he asked.

She stood there fumbling for words in a way that was entirely unlike her. Usually she had an answer for everything on the tip of her sharp tongue.

"You won't tell him, Shamus? Promise?"

He relented a little. "All right, I promise — if you will promise not to go underground any more. It isn't safe. It worries me."

"You're worried about me? Oh, Shamus!"

Lord, he thought, give this kid the least bit of encouragement and she would jump at my neck. Aloud he told her, "Of course I am. I'm worried about you in the same way I'd worry about any friend."

"Oh." Her eyes darkened. "Is that all?"

"Marty, get some sense. Start acting as if you were grown up."

"I am grown up."

"All right. Then prove it to me. Get on your horse and go on home and stop riding around like a headstrong child."

"It's that Dodge woman. You can't see anyone but her."

He did not bother to deny it.

"And I know why you're in Hawthorn. You came up here to hire men. You didn't learn anything last night. You'll just get yourself in trouble, more trouble than you know."

"What are you talking about now?"

She looked miserable, as if she were going to cry. "I can't tell you any more, but please listen to me."

An over-riding impatience mastered him. "Now look, Marty. You're hard enough to get along with without you turning mysterious. Either tell me what you're talking about or shut up."

Some of her old hauteur flashed back into her eyes, but then her mouth softened and she said in a low voice, "Shamus, do you believe that I love you truly?"

"Well," he rubbed his puffed cheek. "I guess you think you do."

"And if a person thinks something hard enough it's true, isn't it?"

"Well, maybe."

"And I saved your life last night, sending the sheriff to the bar?"

"Well, it stopped a fight, I guess."

"Then I'm telling you because I love you that you're being used. I can't tell you who's using you or why, but you've got to believe me. You've got to get out of this country before something terrible happens." She was very intent, very very earnest. "You ride out. You go to California or maybe Arizona, and you write and let me know where you are. I'll come to you, I promise."

He laughed. He could not help it. "Marty, you're priceless." He caught her small shoulders between his hands, leaned forward and kissed her gently on the forehead. "You'd think up some way to trap me if you possibly could. If I did that, I'd be putty in your hands."

Suddenly her small body stiffened and she tore free of his grasp. "Why you great big, overgrown, conceited ape. You're nothing but a big headed saddle tramp. This is the end. You've proved it to me before, but I just wouldn't believe it. I know now. Go ahead, let Myra Dodge make a fool of you, let Tim Younger and Mushy Calder play you for a fall guy. I don't care what happens to you now. I don't care. I don't. Get out."

"Hey wait."

"Get out, before I brain you." She swung the double bitted pick threateningly. From the looks of her she really was set to drive the point into his head.

He backed away. "Now, Marty."

"Get out!" She jumped toward him. He could have grabbed her and wrenched the pick from her grasp, but he was afraid he'd hurt her. He either had to duck out of the building or get brained. He ducked, stumbling, half falling as he slid down the shoulder of the dump toward the street level below.

Halfway down he set his heels to check his progress and looked back. Marty was not following. He turned, searching the hillside to right and left for sight of her small figure. She must have concealed her horse somewhere in the timber above town. But he did not see her and he was certain that she could not have crossed the comparative bareness of the dump so quickly.

"Marty."

There was no answer. A small worry tugged at his mind.

"Marty, answer me."

Still no response.

He stood uncertain for a long minute, staring around; then he turned and began to climb. He came into the old mill and felt the emptiness.

"Marty."

His voice echoed back from the board wall. He looked at the black, blank opening of the tunnel. She had come from there. Maybe she had gone back that way. She could have worked her way down the slippery ladders from one of the shafts, after leaving her horse somewhere far up the mountainside. It made him a little sick, that picture of the girl climbing the rotten rungs with nothing but her tiny light to guide her. The diagram he had seen in the store showed literally miles of drifts and shafts and tunnels. Anyone not familiar with the mine could get lost and wander for days underground.

He started for the tunnel. "Marty!"

The rock walls dampened the sound throwing it back against his ears strangely hushed. Good God, the girl might not hear him with less than a hundred feet separating them.

He tried to run and fell twice, his hands striking down in the damp sludge which had collected in the tunnel floor. There were rails on which the ore cars had once run, and the slippery ties between the rails made tripping easy.

He went on, feeling his way now, glancing across his shoulder, amazed that the opening through which he had entered seemed to have shrunk until it was scarcely larger than a pinhole.

He lost track of time, and was haunted by the fear that he might have passed a ladder in the darkness, a ladder which Marty was even now climbing.

He pushed on, not knowing what else to do, and another disturbing thought came. He had no idea how far he had traveled or where the rock slide was that Crowley had said blocked the tunnel, but it seemed to him that he should have reached it.

The air was growing progressively colder.

He had heard once that mines are warm underground, but this tunnel seemed to hold the chill of the preceding winter.

At last he saw a light far ahead of him. He thought then that he was catching up with Marty, but as he pushed on he realized that the light did not come from her lamp. It was some kind of opening.

He reached it and came out into sunshine, trying to orient himself. He understood slowly that he must have come clear through the ridge, and was now looking down the timbered slope into Pine Valley.

About to turn again, he caught movement far below in the trees. He saw Marty Clare ride across a bare rocky stretch, then lose herself again in the thick stand of pole pine, and two things struck him hard:

First, Ed Crowley had said the drainage tunnel was blocked by a rock slide, yet he had come its full length without finding any obstruction. And second, what was Marty Clare doing on the north side of the ridge?

There were trails through the mountains to the west, narrow, twisting, dangerous trails over which a rider could take a horse with care, but they demanded a hard ride, fifty or sixty miles from Belmont. If Marty wanted to visit the mine, why hadn't she come up through Hawthorn to the old shaft house? It was much shorter, and an easier ride.

Of course, she might not have wanted to be seen on the south side of the ridge and therefore had taken the longer route; or she might not have known where the tunnel opening in Pine Valley led, and wanted to explore it to satisfy her curiosity.

But she had not entered the tunnel by accident. She had come prepared with miner's pick and lamp. He shook his head, still puzzled, standing in the tunnel mouth looking down on the valley.

He didn't know much about the country north of the ridge. It was a barren stretch of territory running sixty or more miles, the land too poor and rough and rocky to attract settlers.

About the only activity in the whole area was the new railroad being pushed westward. He had heard of the big construction camps with their hundreds of graders, bridge men and track layers. He had even been offered a chance to hunt for one of the contractors, since all supplies for the camps came from the East by rail and fresh meat was a continuing problem, but he had not gone.

He turned, peering curiously at the ridge above him. The tunnel had broken through a rock face which slanted upward to lose itself in the snowbank along the crest, still over ten feet deep.

He glanced again at the valley, and then back at the dark tunnel, and the prospect of making the mile-long trip again in darkness brought a little inner shudder.

Yet to climb over the crest was impossible. . . .

Finally he walked to the nearest stand of pole pine. He had no knife, but he managed to tear off half a dozen branches nearly as big as his arm. These he broke again until he had six sections some two feet long. He bound them into two bundles of three sticks each and then built a small fire, laying one of the bundles in the flames so that the ends of the sticks would catch. When the pitch in the wood flamed up he walked into the tunnel, carrying the reserve bundle under his arm.

His makeshift torch sputtered and flared, twice threatened to go out, then continued to burn. The smoky flame lighted the rough rock wall and the slime-covered ties on which the small metal tracks were laid. He bent down once to examine the tracks. It looked as if they had been used fairly recently, for flakes of rust had been knocked

away exposing the brighter metal underneath.

Finally he found the place where the rock
slide had been, and then he was sure. The
bulkhead which had blocked the lower end
of the broken ore chute showed the splintered ends where the wood had split under
the weight from above, releasing tons of
broken ore and rock.

This had all been cleared away, and recently, for some scattered fragments beside
the track were not yet covered by the muck
which coated the damp floor.

He stood motionless, thinking.

Somebody had gone to a great deal of
trouble to remove the rock-slide obstruction, and over there, in a kind of bay which
had been cut into the tunnel wall, he could
see three rusted ore cars. Obviously the cars
had been used to haul the debris away. But
why? Was Ed Crowley right? Was there still
value left in the old mine? Was someone
preparing to reopen it?

11

Shamus Magee emerged from the mine and
slid his way down the loose rock of the
dump to its dusty surface. Night had closed
in on Hawthorn's main street.

Several of the old buildings showed lights, but the store windows were brighter than the rest. He came up onto the porch and walked in. He found a dozen men lined up along the old bar with Ed Crowley acting as his own bartender.

Tim Younger was at one end, and he turned questioning eyes on Shamus, noting the earth stains on his clothes and boots.

"Where have you been?"

"I climbed up to one of the old shafts," Shamus said.

Afterward he wondered why he had not told Younger that he had seen Marty Clare and followed the drainage tunnel through the ridge. It was, he supposed, the puzzle of the missing rock pile which caused his caution — or maybe Marty Clare's investigation of the tunnel — but he did not mean to mention it to anyone until he could talk with Marty again.

"Find any gold?" Younger asked, grinning.

"Didn't look very far. I didn't have a light and the ladder was pretty rotten." He turned as the door opened to let three men come in, and nodded to them.

"Have a drink?"

They came forward, Harvey Taft in the lead. Taft was a big man, slow moving. Until three years ago he had lived in a cabin on

Cow Creek and run a few head of stock there. But Claude Burton had accused him of rustling, burned his cabin and given him twenty-four hours to get out of the valley. No one in Hawthorn hated Burton more bitterly, and Shamus knew it.

After the drinks were served he said, loudly enough for everyone in the room to hear, "How about a job, Harvey? I'm foreman down at the Diamond D and we're hiring."

Taft looked him over carefully. They had never been friends, but Shamus had hunted with him twice. "For that woman, Shamus?"

Shamus held his temper. "For Miss Dodge," he said, and bore down on the "Miss."

Taft seemed to be turning the proposition over in his slow mind. "Burton will run you off. Three of the boys went down there last month. He ran them out."

"We'll have a lot more than three men," Shamus said.

He knew that everyone in the store room was watching him, weighing his words, each deciding for himself what this might mean to him.

"Burton ran you off three years ago, just as he's trying to run Myra Dodge off now. She can use your help."

Taft wiped his mouth with the back of his hand. "No one offered to help me."

Shamus let his eyes range around the room. "I know that." His tone was one of regret. "The southern ranchers might not approve of some of Burton's methods, but they still weren't going to stand against him. And you boys," he included everyone in the building, "weren't organized. That's what I'm offering you — a chance to organize, to fight Burton at his own game."

"And get our necks stretched." Someone at the far end of the counter said this without turning. It brought a laugh, a hollow one.

Shamus' jaw set. He said tightly, "You're all scared. Well, get out of the country then, because there will be no place here for you. Ed Crowley's afraid Burton will burn this town if any of you come to work for me. And let me tell you something. A man like Burton never stops unless he's stopped by someone else. He'll burn you out as sure as I'm standing here. He's only waiting until he thinks the time is right."

Surprisingly Ed Crowley spoke from his place behind the bar. "Magee's right."

Shamus turned to nod thanks to the storekeeper. He had not really expected help from Crowley. The best he had hoped for

136

was neutrality and no objection to his hiring. Maybe an afternoon of thinking had convinced Crowley.

The men at the bar stirred uncertainly, then Taft said, "I'm with Ed. If he says try it, I'll try it. I guess none of us has very much to lose."

A murmur of agreement rose.

"How many men do you want?" Taft said.

Shamus considered. Three riders beside himself, Younger and Calder could do everything necessary at the ranch including the haying, but this was not a case of merely handling the work. He needed enough of a crew to keep Burton off their necks. He said, "Twenty if I can get them," and wondered how long Myra Dodge could maintain a payroll of that size. It was more than the ranch would earn, but if they could recover her cattle and hold out through roundup they could cut the crew back for the winter months.

Suddenly he was very weary. Never had he been called upon to make such decisions.

"You can have forty," Taft told him. "Every man up here would like the chance to take a poke at Burton."

"We can't pay that many, or for that matter feed them."

"All right, pick out the ones you want."

Again Shamus did not know what to do. He did not know the men well enough to judge which would stand under pressure and which might run at the first sign of trouble.

He met Ed Crowley's eyes and had a thought. "I'll leave it up to Ed," he said. "He knows you and you know him. Let him make up a list for me. I'll hire the ones he thinks will want to come, and who won't duck a fight. That is, if he'll do it."

Crowley seemed to consider. "All right." The voice, coming through the tangle of beard, was a hoarse rumble. "I might as well have my hand in this since I'm the one to get hurt. When do you want them?"

"Tonight, tomorrow, as soon as they can come."

"They'll be there. You want something to eat?"

Shamus nodded.

"Stew pot's back in the kitchen. Help yourself."

Shamus turned to look at Younger. The man shrugged. "I ate an hour ago."

Shamus moved on back into the living quarters which Crowley maintained behind the store. He found a plate and filled it from the huge iron pot, then poured himself a cup of coffee and sat down at the wooden drop-leaf table in the corner of the big kitchen.

Tired as he was, he felt that he could lie down on the floor and go to sleep. But he knew he wouldn't. He would ride back to the ranch.

12

Tim Younger brought his horse into Belmont at four-thirty the next morning. He had accompanied Shamus as far as the Diamond D and then, saying he had forgotten some duffle, he had pushed on to town.

Shamus had watched him ride away with mixed feelings. The more he saw of Younger the less he liked the man, and he half expected that Younger had changed his mind, using the duffle merely as an excuse to ride away and not come back.

But Younger meant to come back, and as he urged his horse toward Belmont he whistled softly to himself. Things to his way of thinking were going very well indeed.

He pulled up before the low picket fence which enclosed Dr. Clare's yard and tied his horse. He strolled up the walk, climbed to the low porch and knocked on the door.

After he knocked twice, lamplight flooded

the interior. Dr. Clare's voice asked, "Who is it?"

"Tim."

"What is it now?" Clare sounded annoyed.

"Man hurt, Doc. You'd better take a look at him."

Clare unbolted the door. He had drawn on his pants and was busy fastening his shirt. "How far?"

"Below the livery."

"I'll get my bag." Clare sat down to tie his shoes. "Keep your voice low. My girl's asleep upstairs."

But Marty Clare was not asleep. She lay on the cord bed in her little room under the house's slanting eaves, straining to hear what was said below stairs. Failing, she left the bed. Her small bare feet made no sound on the rough boards as she crept across to peer through a knothole in the floor.

It was not the first time she had used this hole to identify her father's visitors, nor was she surprised when she recognized Tim Younger. The sight of him made her a little ill with dread. Quickly she turned back and slipped into her clothes. The only light in the room came from the moon which filtered through the window in the rear gable.

She finished dressing, padded over to the gable and raised the window. Its sides were carefully soaped so that it made no sound as she hoisted the sash. She had used this means of exit many times before.

Outside, the shed roof slanted above the kitchen. She stepped out onto the shakes and walked sure-footedly to the edge, lowering herself to the cross pieces which ran between the double posts of the trellis for a rose she had been trying to grow.

A moment later she stood in the shadows of the rear yard. She crossed this, vaulted the low fence with the ease of a boy and came out between two buildings. She peered up and down the side street.

Younger had left his horse tethered in front of the house. He and her father were moving along half a block ahead of her. But at the corner, instead of turning up town toward the livery, they cut across the small bridge which spanned the river to the north of town.

Marty followed. Her soundless progress would have done credit to an Indian. In fact her small feet were now encased in a pair of well worn moccasins, and she came to the bridge enbankment just as her father and Younger disappeared beneath its scarred boards. She found her place in the clump of bushes at the far end, knowing from experience that she could overhear everything from there.

Her father's voice was strong and unhurried. "Well, how did it go?"

"Like clockwork. Shamus couldn't have done a better job for us if he'd planned the whole thing. He rode up to Hawthorn this afternoon and then the fool went to take a look at the mine."

"He did?" The doctor's voice lost some of its calm. "He didn't go in the tunnel, did he?"

"No. He climbed to one of the shafts. He didn't have a light anyhow, and if he had, what would he have seen?"

"He might have seen the place where we removed the rock slide."

"What if he had?" Younger's cynical voice sounded a little bored. "At most, all it would have meant to him was that someone was scratching around the old mine, looking for gold that's not there any more. Stop worrying about Magee. The man's a fool — twice as big a fool as he was before that Dodge woman got her hooks on him."

Marty Clare's little hands clenched into tight fists at her sides, and her lips pressed into a tight, angry line.

"He's just what we need," Younger went on. "Nobody ever called him crooked, and now that he's stirred up he'll give Burton the fight of his life. He'll get licked of course. The southern ranchers can't stand by and let Burton get whipped. They'd lose their own grip on the country. But they won't move fast enough. By the time they finally close in on Magee we'll have half the beef in the valley butchered and delivered to the railroad camps."

Clare did not answer and Younger continued. "I've got to hand it to you, Doc. No one else would have figured things out and put everything together — the fact that that tunnel exists, the fact that it could be cleared, and the fact that there were men in Hawthorn to handle the work. You're something of a hero up there, Doc. I didn't get anywhere with Crowley today until I admitted I was working for you. Then he came around to our way of thinking fast."

"I should be a hero," Clare said. "I've taken care of enough of them. If I had a dollar for every worthless life I've saved I wouldn't need to do what I'm doing now."

Younger apparently did not hear him, for he went on. "And Crowley liked the idea of the money he'll get. Do you know what he wants it for? To buy machinery and try to reopen that old mine. The man's crazy. He feels about that mine the way some men feel about a woman. If he had a million dollars he'd sink every cent of it in that empty hole."

Clare said, "I don't care what he does with it, or what any of them do with their share. I want ten thousand dollars. When I have that I'll be content. Anything more you can get is yours."

"Fair enough."

"Can you keep Magee stirred up enough that he won't guess what's going on?"

"Easy. It was a real break for us when things worked out like they did — that Dodge woman showing up and starting her private war with Burton, Burton stealing the grey horse and Magee getting mixed up with them. It would have been a lot tougher to run off those cattle the way we started out, with nothing to cover our tracks."

Clare said, "The difference between a brilliant man and a smart one is that a brilliant man moves fast to take advantage of circumstances. He lets nature work for him. If all these things hadn't happened we would still have gone ahead — but as you say it would have been harder, much more dangerous. Now, if we handle it right, Magee and the Dodge woman will be blamed for everything we do. You get back to the ranch and ride herd on Magee. Don't come in here again unless it's necessary. I'll be out to see you.

One thing about a doctor, his movements are seldom questioned. He's usually on an errand of mercy."

Long after her father and Younger had moved away, Marty Clare sat motionless, concealed from the street by the sheltering bushes. In all of her short life she had never been confronted with a problem of this kind, a decision which involved the two people she cared most about.

To Marty, her father had always been a person apart, a being utterly unlike other men. She had known that he never took her fully in his confidence, but she felt that this was because he considered her yet a child.

She had never known her mother. From earliest memory she and her father had lived on an Army post where he had been the surgeon. Six years ago, he had suddenly resigned and left the post. Why, she did not know and had never dared question. That he should choose to bury himself in this valley, when certainly a man blessed with his ability could have done better in a larger place, was something else with which she had not concerned herself.

She had been content with the freedom the new life had brought her, content to roam at will from one end of the valley to the other.

Only within the last six months had she marked the change in her father, her awareness developing slowly.

First he had begun to discuss the possibility of sending her away to school. She had objected at once, announcing that she had no desire to leave the country. She meant to remain here, and when the time came, to marry Shamus Magee.

And that, she remembered, was one of the few times she had ever seen her father give way to anger. He had called her an empty-headed, immature fool. He had said that Shamus was a useless saddle tramp without a thought in his head beyond the question of his next meal. He had told her that if he ever heard of her having anything to do with Magee, he would personally shoot the good-for-nothing fiddlefoot.

She had been startled by his anger, and by the knowledge that his feeling against Magee went even deeper than his words. She had sensed that he hated Shamus.

This, she decided, was a kind of jealousy, bred of his resentment that anyone else could find a place in her affections, and she might have forgotten it if there had not been other changes in the pattern of her father's life.

For one thing, he had begun seeing a great

deal of Tim Younger. He had never made close association with anyone since coming to Belmont, and that he should single out Younger puzzled her. The two men seemed to have absolutely nothing in common, and the effort they expended to make their meetings seem casual aroused her suspicions.

More than once she had followed her father when he left the house after dark, apparently for an aimless walk. Usually the walk brought him to this bridge, and Younger had met him here.

She had listened then as she had listened tonight, and had been appalled when she realized they were discussing the possibility of stealing cattle from the valley and selling them to one of the commissaries who had the contract for feeding the railroad construction crews.

Gradually the evidence fell into place, and her reluctant mind was forced to accept the fact. The commisary with whom her father was now dealing had run the sutler's store at the Army post where she had been raised — a man named Sorrell, whom she remembered but vaguely.

But she knew no details of the plan, and for these details she set herself to follow both her father and Younger when the chance offered.

Her father roamed the valley almost as widely as she did, calling at the isolated ranches, the few small homesteads spotted along the fringe of the eastern hills, and Hawthorn.

She learned nothing by following him, so she turned her attention to Younger. While trailing him two weeks ago, she had come into Pine Canyon and seen the men working at the mouth of the drainage tunnel.

The activity had made her curious, since Younger had climbed the canyon side and disappeared into the tunnel, remaining in the mountain for the better part of an hour. And later, when she heard Younger and her father discussing this tunnel, she discovered that it had a place in their plans.

Marty Clare had never given much thought to dishonesty. She had grown up alone, with few friends or close acquaintances. She knew that there was a certain amount of cattle rustling in the valley, and disliked the idea of cattle thieves instinctively, and yet it had been a remote feeling, because none of the ranchers involved were her friends.

But the knowledge that her father intended becoming a rustler distressed her. Three times she almost faced him with her discovery and three times lost her courage. Had Magee not been drawn in she might have done nothing about it.

But now Magee was involved. On the night he had come into Belmont in search of a crew she had heard her father tell Younger to be at the saloon, to sign on with the Diamond D, and to use Magee as a front for their operations.

This was why she had stationed herself to intercept Magee before he reached the saloon. She had meant to tell him what she knew, yet somehow at the last minute she had not been able to expose her father.

So she had warned the sheriff, and from there had gone for her horse, and ridden all night to reach Pine Valley.

Hiding on the slope, she had watched the tunnel entrance for two hours to assure herself that no one was around. Then she had climbed the hill, carrying the lamp and miner's pick she had brought with her.

Marty Clare did not frighten easily, and there was little caution in her makeup. The thought of entering that dark mountain alone, with her whereabouts unknown to anyone in the outside world, gave her pause; but she had ridden long, weary miles for that purpose, and if she turned back she would never forgive herself.

Resolutely she lit the small lamp, fastened the cap on her head, and gripping the pick tightly, started into the tunnel. She had heard that you had to be careful exploring abandoned workings because of rattlers, and the tiny flame on her cap threw little light. Yet she pushed on.

The rails and the footprints of the men who had pushed the loaded ore cars gave her a sense of some security. These men who had been in the tunnel when Younger visited them had gone farther into the hill than she. Probably there would be no snakes, and the air was at least breathable.

She reached the point where the ore chute gate had broken and from which the debris had been cleared. It meant little to her and she pressed on. At least there was no turning in the tunnel, no branch passage. Surely she could retrace her steps at any time she chose. It seemed that she had been underground for hours, that she had walked miles. She stopped twice, debating whether to turn back, and twice went ahead.

And then she caught the faint light at the far end that meant some kind of opening. No one in the world was ever more surprised than Marty when she came out into the ruined engine house and saw Shamus Magee.

At first she thought he too had learned of her father's and Younger's maneuvering and had come here to investigate. Then, through a hole in the wall, she saw that she was on the mountainside above Hawthorn.

At once she knew that Magee was there to recruit a crew, and her anger at his stubbornness clouded her thinking for the moment. But after her argument with Shamus, after he had retreated down the hill and she had turned back into the tunnel, the validity of her father's plan became plain to her.

From the first she had wondered how they expected to get the stolen animals out of the valley unobserved, how they hoped to drive them through the long, winding mountain passes and then swing north toward the railroad right of way.

But it would be comparatively simple to drift the stock into the timber at the valley's northern end and work them up the canyon to Hawthorn. No one would see the movement save the people around the old mining town, and none of them had any love for the valley ranches from which the cattle would be taken.

Once through the tunnel, it would be easy to drive the stolen herd on to the railroad and sell them. In a few short days the beef would have been eaten.

The country to the north of the ridge was nearly deserted. Yes, the plan would probably work. She should have told Magee. She could have sworn him to secrecy and told him everything she knew. Maybe he could have figured out a way to stop her father without hurting him.

As she followed the twisting trails she made up her mind to ride out to the Diamond D the first thing in the morning. At least Shamus could fire Younger. At least he wouldn't be blamed for stealing the cattle.

She had gotten home late, and her father was out on some call. Thankfully she fixed herself a little supper and went up to her bedroom, grateful that she did not need to face the doctor that night.

But she was a light sleeper. She heard Doc come in, and it seemed that she had barely closed her eyes again before Younger knocked.

And now, here she sat in the clump of bushes beside the bridge, waiting until she felt certain that her father would be safely in bed, and Younger would be gone.

She rose and made her way along the silent street, noting a full streak of light in the eastern sky. Soon it would be morning.

The house was dark. Younger's horse was not at the rack. She jumped the side fence and cut across the yard. She climbed the trellis to the roof, moving as soundlessly until she gained the window.

She pulled herself over the high sill, dropped lightly into the room beyond, and turned to lower the noiseless sash. Behind her she heard the rasping scratch of a match, and stiffened. There was her father, sitting on the edge of her bed.

He sat for a moment without moving, staring at her in the weak light from the small flame; then he leaned over, lifted the lamp chimney and lit the wick. He replaced the chimney, adjusted the wick, and looked up at her again.

"Where have you been?" he said.

Half a dozen excuses flashed through her mind. She had ridden at night before and he had never doubted what she told him. But now there was something in his manner, a suspicion, which would outlast any lie. And it was better this way.

She said evenly, "I followed you and Tim Younger to the bridge. I listened to you."

13

Dr. Michael Clare had been turned cynical by life. A brilliant student, he had failed to build a proper practice in the East because of his caustic tongue and his refusal to cater to patients who had more money than illness. His wife had died leaving him with a baby girl, and in desperation he had sought the security promised by the Army, signing on as surgeon.

But the regulations, the petty jealousies, the constant friction between the personalities had been too much for him. He had stood it for nearly ten years and finally, hearing that the only doctor in Belmont had died, he had resigned and brought his daughter to this valley to start life over again.

And now he was going to die. He needed no one to verify his diagnosis. The lump was there, the pain which he tried to control with whisky and laudanum was increasing. At most he allotted himself six months, and in that six months he had to make some provision for Marty.

Watching her now he thought again how very like her mother she was — the same red hair, the same wild, carefree way, the same intent preoccupation with things which interested her.

She was not like other people. She was a wild spirit, as yet untamed, as yet not stagnated by forces around her. He thought sadly that that would come in time. Responsibilities and trouble, life itself would finally force her to conform to the pattern which society had set up for all.

But he wanted her to retain her freedom as long as possible, to have a chance to see more of this world than the remote, high valley in which they lived.

That would take money, and he had spent many nights alone, trying to figure the answer to his problem. His meeting with Sorrell came by chance. A man had been hurt at one of the grading camps and he had been summoned. Sorrell and he had never been friends, but the ex-sutler welcomed him as if they were lost brothers. In the course of their talk Sorrell had mentioned his immense difficulty in securing fresh meat for the four thousand men he fed daily. It was then that Dr. Clare decided to rustle cattle.

He justified the plan by telling himself that practically everybody in the valley owed him money. A doctor is always the last to be paid, and he knew that many of his bills would never be collected.

Until he found Tim Younger the whole thing had been merely a vague idea. It was Younger who thought of the drainage tunnel, Younger who explained that they could not hope to drive stolen stock over the mountain trails.

"But you can't push cattle through a mile of tunnel," Clare had objected. "As spooky as they are they'd never enter it."

"We don't have to," Younger said. "We drive them up to Hawthorn, maybe a hundred at a time. We butcher them in the old mill building and toss the hides and heads and entrails down one of the old sumps, and dump rock on top of them. We move the meat in the ore cars through the tunnel and load it onto your man's wagons in Pine Valley."

"It's twenty-five or thirty miles to the camps. In this weather it will spoil before it gets there. That's Sorrell's trouble now."

Younger snorted. "With a hundred million tons of snow and ice still on the ridge?"

Clare had laughed, then. Everything seemed to be shaping up perfectly, as if the whole action had been planned by providence. And then to have the trouble spring up between Burton and Magee . . . now there was an extra dividend on which they had not counted!

The fact that Shamus Magee probably would be blamed for the rustling only added to Doc Clare's pleasure. He hated Magee. He did not recognize the root of his hate, but it was based on envy — always he had

156

dreamed of having the carefree freedom which Shamus Magee took for granted, and never had circumstances allowed him to attain it. And on top of this, Marty's liking for the man rankled him. He wanted something better for his daughter than a riding tramp who owned nothing except the saddle he sat in.

Shamus could be caught and hanged, for all of him. Everything had appeared so easy half an hour ago, as he stood talking with Younger under the bridge. And now. . . .

Dr. Michael Clare read the stubborn determination in his daughter's face, and wondered what he could say to her. He knew her well enough to understand that there was no compromise in her nature. The argument that he was about to die and needed money for her security would have no effect on her.

He said, "You heard everything?"

"Everything," she said steadily. "I followed Younger the other day. I saw the men working at the tunnel in Pine Canyon. I went through it yesterday."

This was worse than he had thought, but his mind, always at its best in times of stress, was already working on this new problem. He said, "What are you going to do?"

"Go to the sheriff unless you promise to

stop. Unless you call off Younger and the men."

He stood up and paced back and forth across the room. The pain was worse tonight. Finally he turned to her. "What can I say?"

She was staring at him, stricken. Nothing like this had entered her life before. "Why, Father? Why?"

He passed a thin hand wearily across his eyes. "Who knows why a man changes his ways? The chance came. I took it. I guess that's all there is."

"And what are you going to do now?"

He had a hasty plan. It involved several complications, but it should work out. He would go ahead, he had to go ahead. There was no turning back. As soon as he got his share of the money for the meat he would forward it to a friend, the only friend he had in the world, a man with whom he had gone to school. He knew this man thoroughly, and felt that he could trust him. He would explain everything in the letter, and ask that after his death this man come forward with an offer to take Marty, to educate her at his own expense. The ten thousand could be used for that, but Clare dared not leave it directly to Marty, knowing full well that she would return it to the people from whom the cattle were stolen.

"What can I do?" he asked, and gave her a small smile. "You are my conscience and now that you know, I can't go ahead."

He could be charming when he chose, and her love for him was deep, too deep to be completely denied at anytime. She felt a sudden rush of tenderness, a desire to put her arms about him, to comfort him. But she restrained this, saying, "You'll call Younger off?"

"Of course. But first there is something else I have to do. I have to tell Sorrell. He depends on this beef. He doesn't know it was to be stolen."

This last was a lie. The commissary knew perfectly well that the meat would be stolen, and did not care. The price he had agreed to pay was less than half what meat would have cost him shipped in by work train.

She studied his face, wanting to believe, yet not quite sure. "You'll do it, now, at once? You promise?"

"Of course," he said with a sudden boyishness, "but I can't blame you for doubting me after what's happened. Tell you what, Marty. Come with me. Ride to the construction camps, and then we'll swing back and tell Younger the deal is off. He can't go ahead unless I arrange the sale of the meat for him."

That convinced her. Tired as she was, she wanted to get started. At first light, they left the house and saddled their horses and headed across the valley toward the western hills.

Marty had never been in the construction camps, but she had watched the men from the distant hills as they ran out the lang grading teams before the track layers arrived. She was amazed at the size of the main camp, almost a town under canvas, with its saloons, its gambling halls, its long rows of bunkhouses.

The Pacific Northern Railroad had profited from the experience gained by previous lines. The builders did not concern themselves with townsites or developing the country through which the road passed, but concentrated on opening up a direct line from the booming northwest into the Chicago area.

Ben Sorrell had run sutlers stores at a dozen Army posts. He had traded with the Indians in the Southwest. But he had never found anything as profitable as this contract to feed four thousand men in the grading camps.

His wife Florence stood six feet tall and had a voice with the harsh overtones of a man's. In some ways she was more a man than Sorrell, and she ran the business with an iron hand, bossing the twenty Chinese cooks and waiters with the ruthlessness of a drill sergeant.

The crews were tough, mostly Irish, fresh off the boats, with no respect for God or devil. But they did not fight in the mess hall. They created no disturbance of any kind. Every Paddy in camp had a wholesome respect for Florence Sorrell, and the stories about her ranged from the time she had laid a foul-mouthed foreman out with an iron skillet, to the occasion when three men had attempted to hold up the paycar and received varying patterns of buckshot from her double-barreled gun.

The doctor talked to Florence rather than to Sorrell, for the decision would be hers. He had known her from his Army days and recognized that she was boss of the family.

Marty sat outside in the dining room, eating a belated dinner. He had excused himself to come into the commissary office.

"That's the way it is," he told Florence Sorrell. "My daughter knows all about the plan to steal the cattle and she's raising hell. I'm supposed to be here to tell you that we won't go through with it."

Ben Sorrell twisted his fingers nervously.

He stood less than five feet ten and weighed only a hundred and fifty pounds. "Look, Doc." His voice had a kind of whining note. "We've got to have that meat."

"You'll get it."

"But you said —"

"I said I was supposed to tell you. What I actually came for was to bring Marty. I don't want her hurt, but I do want Florence to keep her here until this is over. You should be able to manage that all right. No one need know anything about it but a couple of your China boys, and they don't even speak the language so anyone can understand."

Sorrell spread his hands. "We can't do that, Doc. Why, hell, she'll talk sure after she gets free, and we would be in the soup."

"She won't talk," Clare promised him. "Once it's done she couldn't say a word without having me sent to prison or hung, and Marty would never do that. Besides, she has no proof that you know the meat is stolen. You can always blame the whole thing on Younger and me. There's no way of tracing the cattle to you. The hides and heads will be buried deep in the mine and we'll block the tunnel again as soon as we finish. A bunch of powder will take care of that."

He sat back, aware that he had said enough. The rest was up to Florence Sorrell, and he had long ago gauged her. Greed ruled her spirit, and unless they kept Marty a prisoner the Sorrells would have no cheap meat to sell. He listened to them argue back and forth and finally, after the woman won, he stood up.

"There's one thing," he said harshly. "I don't want her misused. I want her kept here, but I don't want anyone to punish her in any way. If I find out you have, I'll go to the railroad people and make a clean breast of everything. I'll swear that both of you were in the business from the start."

Florence said, "You don't have to threaten us, Doc. I remember the girl as a kid. I wouldn't see her hurt."

Clare walked to the dining room door called, "Come in here a minute, Marty."

She came, unsuspecting. Not until he had told her that she was staying with the Sorrells for a while did she realize what had happened. She turned on him then, her green eyes flashing. "I'll never trust you again, Doc."

He winced inwardly. His physical pain was easier to bear than the pain of her scorn.

"You can't hold me forever," she told him. "You'll be sorry when I get loose — and if anything happens to Shamus Magee I'll kill you."

14

Shamus Magee wondered at the satisfaction he found in his new situation. All his life he had ducked authority and responsibility, and here he was actually enjoying the sense of power that came from directing the activities of the ranch.

For two days the new crew straggled in. He put them to work as soon as they arrived, repairing the fences, cleaning the buildings. All during this time he had Mushy Calder scouting to the south, watching for any move by Burton's men. It was strangely quiet and the quiet worried him.

On the fourth morning he marshaled his men, twenty-one of them, counting Younger, and rode directly for the Bar X home ranch, leaving Mushy Calder as guard for the Diamond D.

Younger protested the move, but Shamus said flatly, "The Diamond D stock is on Bar X grass where Burton put it. We're taking it off, but I'm not going to stand the chance that he'll claim we took some of his critters along with ours. I'm giving him an opportunity to send his reps with us while we cut the herd."

"He won't let you do it."

"He won't stop us," Shamus said, and rode on, humming at first, then singing softly to himself.

The lonesomest cowboy
That ever was known
Ate garlic for breakfast
And rode all alone.

Younger spoke with a trace of weariness. "Don't you know any other song?"

"I like that one. If you don't, drop back."

Younger dropped back, and they came down the lane into the Bar X with Shamus well in advance of his bunched riders. Claude Burton stood on the porch of the main house with Bud Cole at his side. Half a dozen members of the crew were scattered around the big yard as if accidentally halted in some chore. Shamus held up his hand.

Younger passed on the signal. The riders behind him spread out into a fan-shaped half circle. Younger kept coming, a thin smile on his long, dark, handsome face.

Burton said, "Get off the ranch, Magee."

"We will," Shamus told him, "after we round up the Diamond D stock you stole."

"I didn't steal them. I bought them."

"May I see your bill of sale?"

Nothing else he could have said would have infuriated Burton half as much. The string of curse words that poured out of him would have done credit to a bo'sun. Shamus took no notice, letting the volume die when Burton fell silent for want of breath.

Then he said, still in a reasonable tone, "I don't want trouble with you. If you'd rather have your crew round up our stock and bring them home than have me cut through your herd, just say so."

Burton drew a long, tortured breath. "The first man who tries to drive a steer off this range gets hung, and that's a promise." He took another breath and raised his voice to a bull-like roar.

"You hear that, you bunch of scurvy brush-jumpers? I've stood the last I'm going to stand from any of you. Ride out. You're a bunch of thieves. You're as bad as the woman you're riding for, and this time I'm not going to forget it. If I catch any of you in this country again you'll hang."

Younger laughed and the sound further infuriated Burton. Shamus said quickly, "You'd better listen to me, Claude. I'm the only man here who wouldn't like to see you dancing at the end of a rope. I'm not looking for trouble. I just want the Diamond D cattle, and I'm going to take them. You can send reps with us or not, as you choose."

For an instant he thought that Burton would go for his gun. Then with visible effort the rancher got control of himself. He said darkly, "This isn't the end, Magee. This is only the beginning. Now get out of my yard."

They rode out under the sullen eyes of Burton's crew. Once clear of the lane Shamus halted his men. "We've got to move fast. Burton is going to get help. He didn't back down this morning, he's just waiting. I want every Diamond D steer combed out and I don't want any Bar X beef scattered in by mistake. Is that clear?"

They watched him, their expressions unreadable. Behind his back Tim Younger winked.

Shamus said, "Younger, take fifteen men and ride to Burton's southern line. Spread out and work back this way. Don't miss them in the brush or draws."

Younger nodded.

"I'll start from here and drift anything we find west away from his buildings. That way I can keep an eye on what he's doing. If he starts moving men toward us I'll send a rider to you."

Younger rode away with his men, and

once clear of Shamus he told them, "We'll pick up the Diamond D stuff, but we'll also drift the Bar X stock into the hills. Don't mix them. The boys from Hawthorn will be down to pick the Bar X stuff from the brush and drive it up to the mine tonight."

They nodded, spreading out into a long line and starting their gather.

From a mile away, Shamus kept a close watch on the Burton ranch. He saw no sign of any riders coming in his direction, but he did see a trace of dust above the trail which led south to Belmont. That meant Burton was hunting reinforcements.

By a little after noon, his five riders had gathered nearly a hundred head of steers which bore the sprawling Diamond D, and began working them west and a little north to meet the main gather which was coming up from the south.

Taft was riding next to Shamus. Suddenly he said, "Company."

Shamus turned in the saddle and saw a single rider angling toward him across the rolling grassland. He motioned Taft and the others to go on and pulled his horse around, waiting for the oncoming rider to reach him.

While the man was still an eighth of a mile away he recognized Luke Ronson. The sheriff held to his easy pace and finally reined in.

"Kind of off your range, aren't you, Shamus?"

Magee did not answer and Ronson squinted at him. "Burton give you permission to comb his land?"

"You know he didn't."

"That's not very smart."

Shamus tried to curb his rising impatience. "Burton moved this stock down onto his place. In my book that's rustling. I don't know what you'd make it."

"He claims he bought it," Ronson said tiredly. "He claims it belongs to him just as much as if it had Bar X burnt on its flank."

"I know what he claims. Ask him for a bill of sale."

"We been all over that."

"I know we have, which is the point I make. The cows are here and Burton isn't going to take them back to where he got them. I gave him that chance, so what choice have I got except to come and get them myself?"

"You could have got a court order."

"The circuit rider only gets here every six weeks and he was here two weeks ago. Figure it out. By the time I got an order and you executed it Burton could have these doggies clear out of the country. No thanks,

Luke. We'll just take them home now."

"Mind if I take a look at the brands?"

"Help yourself."

Ronson said, "I don't like doing this, Shamus, but I don't like a range war either, and that's just what you're building. Burton sent Cole and three other riders down to the southern ranchers to demand help. He'll get it, too."

"Let him."

"You're kind of pig-headed aren't you? How many men you got?"

"Enough."

"I doubt it. If the men south of town take chips in the game you'll have fifty guns against you."

"Ronson, get this through your head. We're in this fight to stay. I'll have most of these cattle back on home range tonight. I've got twenty men who haven't a thing to lose and who hate Burton in the bargain, and there are twenty or thirty more up in the canyon just hoping I'll hire them. If Burton attacks the Diamond D he'll get his belly full. Just tell him that. And tell the men south of the town they'd better understand the game before they buy chips. Now, if you want to take a look at the herd, go ahead."

He sat tight, letting the sheriff ride forward

alone, watching Ronson as he snaked back and forth through the bunched animals. An hour later the sheriff rode away, so he pushed his gather on to join the larger bunch which Younger's men were bringing up from the south.

By dinner time they were well north of Burton's place, not more than five miles from the unmarked boundary of the Diamond D range.

He had hoped to be on the home ranch by dark, and he pushed them hard, estimating that they must have six or seven hundred head in the combined gather. It was as good as he could expect to do at the moment. With cattle scattered over half a million acres of range, fast-working riders were bound to overlook some strays. But the drive went too slowly.

Younger eased himself in his saddle, cocking a leg around the horn while he built a cigarette.

"We'll never make it," he said. "They're riled up now. If we don't start bedding them down soon we'll never hold them tonight."

Shamus knew he was right. He turned, squinting toward the rising mountains less than two miles to the west of them. "If they ever got in that brush we'd have the devil's own time digging them out. Let's move on to the next creek. Send someone over to the ranch to bring some grub back. The boys will have to wait to eat until maybe midnight. Get the stock bedded down and set guards out. I don't want to be surprised."

Younger said, "You going someplace?"

"Back toward Burton's a way, just in case." He swung his horse and rode off. Younger watched him go, smiling faintly. Then he beckoned to Taft.

"Take four men, cut out a hundred head and start them for the canyon. You'll have a moon tonight and you should be able to handle that many. Burgess and Sawyer will meet you in the canyon with some men to take them on up. Tell them to start butchering as soon as they get to the mill. The wagons for the first load will be in Pine Valley tomorrow noon."

Shamus rode steadily. The country rolled, so that in places you could see several miles, in others less than a hundred yards.

The sun disappeared behind the mountains at his back and the shadows grew longer until the whole valley floor merged into darkness. It was an hour yet to moonrise, and he picked up the lights of the distant ranch long before the moon lifted above the trees.

Also, before he had topped the last rise, he sensed activity in the Bar X yard. He pressed closer, seeing the extra horses tied to the corral fence and men streaming in and out of the cook house. He left his horse, moving forward on foot. He judged that Cole and the other Bar X emissaries had brought reinforcements from the south, and his mouth set grimly.

From a point behind the hay barn he watched Burton come out onto the porch. The yard was lighted by a dozen lanterns. He had no trouble making out Cole and Burton, but he could not hear what they said.

He did not need to hear. They were primed for attack. He faded back to his horse and swung into the saddle. He had to warn Younger. Somehow they had to hold off the attackers before they reached the cattle. Otherwise his crew's work would be for nothing. The animals would be stampeded, scattered through the timbered foothills to the west.

But still he lingered. He could not believe that they knew exactly where the cattle were being held. They would separate and search across the valley.

And then he saw the men mounting. They were not coming toward him, however. They were heading out the long lane to the road.

Caught by surprise, he wondered frantically what they were up to. Then he understood Burton's intentions. He should have forseen this. He should have known from Burton's former tactics how the man's mind would work.

Burton didn't have to worry about the Diamond D stock. No matter what happened, they would remain in the valley and he could round them up at his leisure. What bothered him was the Diamond D ranch itself. This was the headquarters, the rallying place for the riders Shamus had brought down from Hawthorn. If Burton could destroy it, if he could recapture Myra Dodge, the crew would drift off, each man trying to save himself.

Shamus' first thought was to go after the crew, but nearly fifteen miles stretched between him and the pocket where Younger and the men were holding the restless cattle. Long before he could get them and return to the ranch, the log buildings would go up in flames.

He turned north, paralleling the road, driving his horse as fast as he could. But the land was rough, cut by half a dozen brush-lined creeks which swept out of the mountains and twisted across the valley to join the Belmont.

After a couple of miles he realized that he could not make it in time. He had to slow too often, to detour around marshy places along the creeks. He changed direction, angling out to the road, knowing he would not be in time to save the ranch but swearing that they would not carry off Myra Dodge again as long as he lived.

He reached the trail a mile behind the bunch who rode with Burton, and turned into it. His horse had been going all day. It began to show signs of strain and he eased off the pace. He could not hope to catch the Bar X riders and he might need the animal badly before this night ended.

He had no way of telling how many men Burton had, but it only made sense that the rancher would not move without sufficient strength to equal the Hawthorn men who had followed Shamus that morning.

He rode on grimly. The ranch was not far ahead. Suddenly the flat whanging sound of a distant rifle shot split the night. A dozen other shots answered it. He guessed Mushy Calder had spotted them and fired, and they had fired back at him.

He had forgotten Mushy. But by god, when you left Mushy on guard he stayed on guard. The firing was general now, and in his mind's eye he could visualize the scene. Part of it, anyhow. The attackers would have spread out to cover the buildings from all sides. Mushy Calder would be crouching on the roof, or holed up in the main house, or maybe hiding in one of the outbuildings. It did not really matter. In time they would dig him out. Claude Burton was not one to be halted by a single man.

Well, Mushy Calder could take his chances and care for himself. Mushy was too old a hand not to have realized from the beginning where all this could lead. But Myra. . . . She was new to this country, and a woman. Would Burton's riders take into consideration that she was probably in the house? Would they hold their fire? Or even if they did, a stray bullet might catch her.

He reached the mouth of the lane. Fire licked up from one of the hay stacks to the right of the barn, and a crouched figure ran backward away from the stack, seeking shelter.

From the barn a rifle flashed and the crouching figure stumbled and went down. So Mushy was in the barn. Shamus knew it as surely as if he had seen the little wolfer fire the shot. At once a dozen rifles cut loose from all directions, aimed at the barn, their slugs tearing into the old logs, hammering against the closed double doors, splintering the window frames.

Shamus rode forward, jerking his rifle from its boot. He had no real hope of hitting anyone. He just wanted to cause a diversion. Suddenly he saw a man on horseback move in the darkness on his left, and someone called to him, words he could not understand.

He fired point blank. The figure slumped and the horse ran riderless across the yard, directly toward the burning stack. All around him the night burst into life, men shouting at each other, calling their warning in the gloom.

He pulled his tired horse around. A gun flashed behind him, the bullet a whisper through the night air to his left. He did not try to escape. He drove his mount straight at a group of men who loomed up before him, firing as he came, knowing that they would hesitate to return his fire because of their friends behind him.

They split. Someone tried to grab the bridle rein and he clubbed the man from the saddle with his rifle barrel. Then he was through them, driving around a corner of the house with shots ripping the night behind him. Near the corral four men appeared. They did not fire, not certain who he was. Their very numbers made for confusion and saved him. He rode the first man down and saw the others turn to dive for safety below the corral rails. He swung around the enclosure, plunging among the horses they had left there.

He cleared his saddle in an instant, yanking loose the tie rope of the first horse he came to and swinging up into that saddle.

Behind him the yard was in turmoil. He hoped that in the excitement Mushy would manage to make his escape, and with this in mind he pulled around to the left. The burning stack revealed scattered figures running across the yard, but did not furnish enough light to outline him plainly as a target. And then he saw the figure dive from the barn's rear window and run toward the line of brush which marked the creek. He rode after it, calling Mushy's name.

Calder reached the brush, saw the rider charging at him, and raised his rifle. He let it drop as he recognized Shamus' voice. A second later Magee hauled up beside Mushy. He kicked one foot loose from the stirrup, reached down to catch Calder's wrist, and swung the little man up behind him. Then he drove his spur into the horse. It leaped forward, almost raking them from its back as it charged through the brush, jumped the creek and clawed its way up the far bank. Behind them he heard scattered shots and the drum of running horses.

"Myra," he yelled at Mushy. "Where's Myra Dodge?"

"She got away." Mushy was twisting to shoot back at their pursuers. "I had a horse ready. She rode out for help when I heard them coming."

15

Mushy Calder had estimated with fair accuracy the spot in which the herd would be bedded down. The old wolfer knew every inch of the valley as well as he did the lines on his sunburned hands.

"They won't make the ranch tonight," he told Myra Dodge before sundown. "If they were coming in we'd have seen them by now. They'll bed down and hold them, probably on Cow Creek."

All day he had been nervous as a cat, watching the trail, riding out half a dozen times to high ground, searching for any sign of Burton's men.

As the sun sank he had saddled a horse and tied it to the corral fence. "If we hear someone coming," he said, "you climb on and ride out."

"What about you?" Myra asked. Not that she cared about his safety, but she liked to understand exactly what was going on.

Calder had been considering this himself all afternoon. "I'll be all right," he said. "If it's dark I can slip out of the barn and make the cover along the creek. Those fools will never catch me then."

But he had misjudged one thing. He had not counted on a number of Burton's men cutting around the corral and thus nearly plugging his means of escape. If Shamus had not distracted them he would not have made it.

But Myra Dodge knew nothing of this. She rode westward as soon as the sound of Burton's approach reached the ranch. She rode hard, coming to Cow Creek and turning to follow it toward the hills. And then she met the rider who had been sent home after food, and told him of Burton's attack.

At once he said, "We'd better tell Younger." He cut away from the creek, leading her northward for two miles, until they came upon five men driving a hundred cows.

Younger heard them coming and reined back to intercept them. The sight of Myra made him furious, and for her part Myra Dodge was no fool. She could tell that this was not the main herd. This stock was not being driven toward the ranch, and every cow bore the Diamond D brand.

But she gave no sign while the other riders could overhear her. Instead she told Younger about the attack.

Younger received the news with mixed emotions. He did not care what happened to the ranch, but if Burton had enough men to risk the raid, he might decide to continue on up the canyon to Hawthorn and clean out the old mining camp for once and all.

And if they met Burton's bunch in the canyon with the stolen beef they might have difficulty explaining it away.

A plan shaped itself in his mind. If Burton could attack the Diamond D, what was to stop them from raiding the Bar X? He turned to the grub-carrier who had come with Myra Dodge.

"Ride back to the herd," he said. "Tell Taft to leave three men with the cows, and the rest of you head for Burton's. I'll meet you there."

He heard Myra Dodge draw her breath sharply and grinned in the darkness. Tim Younger had known many women, and he had taken the measure of the Diamond D owner at their first meeting.

"You mind?" he asked.

For a moment she was silent. Then her voice, coarsened by feeling, reached him. "Not if it will hurt Burton."

"It will hurt Burton." He swung his horse around, riding to where his men held the hundred head. "You boys take them on to the timber, but don't take them into the canyon until you hear from me." He did not bother to explain, but turned again to the girl. "You going along?"

He heard her chuckle. "I wouldn't miss it for anything in the world. Anything that hurts Burton makes me happy."

"You're not alone," he said. "Every man who rides with us feels the same way. A lot of them will have more self respect when they see the Bar X go up in smoke."

He put his horse into motion and she swung in beside him. "I hate to make the point, Mr. Younger, but those are my cattle your men are driving into the timber."

"Are they?" His tone expressed good natured doubt.

She stared hard at him in the thin moonlight. "What do you mean by that?"

"I'm not Shamus Magee. I don't think everything in petticoats is holier than a nun. I've heard the story about Burton's stolen bill of sale. Claude Burton may be a bastard, but he's not a liar."

The darkness hid her flush.

"So let's be sensible," he said. "You and I are a lot alike. We don't care who gets hurt as long as it isn't us. You want something, so do I. You're trying to get the Diamond D ranch. Believe me, that's wrong. It's wrong because the valley would never let you hold it."

"You have a better idea?" she said waspishly.

"Yeah, I have. I have a way of turning the cattle in this valley into gold, and gold is something you can carry in your saddlebags. I don't give a damn about Burton, or the men he's run out of their homes. All I'm interested in is how much money I can take away from here."

"Then why are you riding to the Bar X?"

He grinned, knowing that she could not see his change of expression in the poor light. "I don't want Burton riding up to Hawthorn. I want to keep this valley in an uproar with no man trusting his neighbor. That's the only way I can operate, and when it's all over, you and I can ride out of here and the boys and Magee will get the blame."

"And how do I know," she said slowly, "that when you ride out I'll be with you?"

"Have you looked in a mirror lately?"

No other answer would have convinced

her as fully. Her ruling passion was vanity, a certainty of her good looks, of her power to control men. She laughed.

"Younger, why didn't I meet you before I met Magee?"

"Lucky you didn't. We need him. He's fighting for a lady. He'll fight hard, and while he's fighting we'll steal every head we can lay our hands on."

He rode on, and she was content to follow. Had she known Younger's mind, she would not have been so happy. Tim Younger cared nothing for anyone except himself. He would use Dr. Clare as long as the doctor could help him. He would use Shamus and the men from Hawthorn, and he would use Myra Dodge.

They met the men from the holding herd two miles below the Burton ranch, and he shaped up the situation quickly. "Burton is having himself some fun burning the Diamond D. If you'll take a look you can see the glow in the sky."

Several of them shifted in their saddles.

"Well give him something to think about. What's good enough for the Diamond D is good enough for the Bar X. Burton likes fire. He burned a lot of you out. Now we can repay the compliment."

They leaned toward him, eager now.

"And when we finish, half of you go back to the herd and move it to the timber toward the canyon mouth. The rest of you scatter. From now on you're working on your own. Drift Burton's stock into the hills. Don't get yourselves caught. You'll be safe enough if you'll watch. He hasn't got the strength to run you all down.

"I'll be at the canyon with the rest of the Hawthorn men. It's narrow. We can hold it against an army. Get the stock that far, and I'll see that it's taken up to the mine and butchered. Come on, let's ride."

They rode with mounting enthusiasm. Every man in the party had a personal score to settle with Claude Burton. Some had nursed their hate for years, until it had festered inside of them.

Younger rode in the lead, the girl at his side. He said, "Every man will load as much food as he can carry from the storehouse before we burn it. It will give you something to eat for the next few days."

She glanced at him. "Did you mean it — can you hold the canyon?"

He smiled. "Ever been up to Hawthorn?"

"Once."

"Then you know how narrow it is. Half a dozen men high on the walls could keep a full company of cavalry from getting to

185

Hawthorn. We'll hold the place until we get as many cattle as we can butchered and sold, then you and I will fade away and leave the rest to face the valley ranchers."

"But how do we get out? How do we get the beef out? That canyon is a box."

He told her about the drainage tunnel and she laughed. "That's smart. But what about Magee?"

"What about him?"

"He's honest. He'll never stand for this."

"What can he do?"

She said nothing, but her silence did not mean agreement. She had a feeling about Magee. It seemed to her that Younger underrated him. She meant to wait, to watch and to be very, very careful.

They came into the yard from all sides, spread out and alert, but there was no defense. The place was deserted save for the Chinese cook and they caught him flat-footed, thinking it was Burton returning.

Younger put him on a horse and sent him out to give Burton the news. He wanted the rancher to know that the Bar X was being fired. He wanted Burton to turn back and ride for the charred ranch, and if he failed to see the light from the blazing buildings, the Chinaman would bring him.

Then, systematically, they looted the store

room, taking everything that could be put to their use. In the main house one man discovered the iron-bound chest which Burton kept because he had little trust in banks, and smashed its lock with a shot.

His resulting howl of joy brought most of the crew running. The chest held nearly seven thousand dollars in gold. Younger drew his gun and forced them to divide it equally.

This he did not relish. Had he known about the chest he would have tried to keep it for himself. But it was too late, unless he wanted mutiny on his hands. He superintended the division, then gave the orders to light the buildings.

And the leaping flames guided Mushy Calder and Shamus Magee to the Bar X.

They had been cutting southwest across the valley after picking up the grey stallion, which Mushy had hidden in a canyon behind the Diamond D.

Magee was riding the grey. Calder loved the stallion, but since he was not horseman enough to handle such a half broken brute, he had settled for the horse Magee had grabbed from the corral fence. They were on their way to rejoin the men with the herd when they saw the fire, far to the east.

Magee reined in, studying it, orienting himself. "The Bar X."

Mushy Calder chuckled. "That should teach Burton not to play with matches."

"But who's burning it?"

"What difference does it make?"

To Magee it made all difference in the world. He had been fighting Burton, but trying to do it within the law. All he wanted was to get the Diamond D stock back onto the Dodge range and hold them there. If Burton chose to attack him, he would at least be in a strong legal position But to burn the Bar X? The fact that Burton had already burned the Diamond D did not justify the act in the light of the law, and he knew that the southern ranchers would side with Burton.

"Let's have a look." He spurred the grey toward the ranch. The horse was fresh and full of run, and he outdistanced Calder so badly in the first half mile that the wolfer hauled up.

"Hell with him," he muttered, swinging his horse around and heading back toward Bear Creek. Mushy Calder had no feeling about the law, and he could see little reason to exert himself to save Burton property.

Shamus raced on. Even in his preoccupation with the night's events he could not ignore the lift that the horse gave him. Never in his life had he ridden anything like this stallion. There must be a trace of racing blood back in its pedigree somewhere. It was big, powerful, and it had heart.

He let it go, knowing that any attempt to check it would only mean a tussle between them. The tireder it grew the more easily it could be handled.

But the horse was smarter than he realized. It dawned on him that it had stopped fighting the bit, that it had set its own pace, a pace faster than he would have expected, yet one which the grey could hold a long time.

They heard him coming long before he hit the yard, and he made no effort at concealment. He saw Younger and Myra Dodge plainly in the light of the rushing flames, standing before the main house.

Younger! He had left Younger in charge of the herd. What was he doing here?

He rode in, checking the grey within a few feet of Myra and Younger. He said, "Whose idea was this?"

Younger stood with his feet wide apart and Shamus could make out a smile on his face. "What's the difference?" Younger said.

"This difference," Shamus said. "There can be only one boss in anything. Climb on your horse and ride out. You're through."

Younger did not move. He just stood there, right hand hanging easily below his holstered gun.

"Maybe you'd better tell him," he said to Myra.

Shamus did not make the mistake of taking his eyes from Younger's face.

"Tell me what?" he demanded.

"*You're* through," Myra Dodge said distinctly. "I've appointed Tim foreman."

16

Shamus Magee sat quietly in the saddle letting the meaning of Myra's words seep into his consciousness.

"Why'd you do that?" he asked finally.

She came forward and in the firelight, and all of the softness he remembered was gone now. She said, "Look, Magee, from the first you've held back in this fight. If you want it in plain words, you aren't tough enough to stand up to Burton. Would you have burned this place?"

He wiped his hand slowly across his face. "It was a damn fool thing to do."

"Would you have?"

"No. You'll turn the sheriff against you. You'll turn everyone against you." He was trying to be patient, to reason with her, while a vagrant part of his mind wondered what Younger had said, what arguments the man had used. "Before this we had legal grounds to stand on."

"When did Claude Burton ever care about legal grounds?"

"And we might have had the sympathy of a lot of valley people, as long as we were the wronged parties, as long as we were merely trying to get back your stock and hold your ranch. Now, when the sheriff finds out he can't handle things, he'll appeal to the territorial governor to send in U.S. marshals. We'll be fighting Burton and the law. Don't go ahead this way, Myra. You'll lose the ranch, everything."

"Are you finished?"

Her face looked almost ugly in the harsh light. He stared at her as if she were a stranger. Then he said in a tired voice, "Yes, I guess I'm finished."

"All right. Ride out."

He glanced around the yard. The men were eating, some standing by their horses, others mounted, gnawing at cold biscuits and jerked meat they had stolen from the cook shack.

These men he had recruited from the canyon, and he felt a certain responsibility for their being here. If it had not been for him they probably would have stayed in the security of Hawthorn.

"What about it? Who's going to ride with me?"

They looked at him and away, their faces expressionless, without interest. Every man had more gold in his saddlebags than he had ever expected to own, plus Younger's promise that the northern end of the valley would be stripped of cattle and Claude Burton would be ruined.

He recognized his defeat and turned back to the girl. He did not hate her. In fact he felt sorry for her, because Tim Younger must have misled her in some way. The warmth, the heady excitement she used to arouse was dead in him now, but still he acknowledged a certain responsibility toward her. . . .

And out there, down the road, he could hear the drum of many hoofs. Burton coming home, an angry Burton, ready to hang anybody he caught this night, including Myra Dodge.

Already the dismounted men in the yard had swung up into their saddles, already they were turning away as if each cared only for his own safety.

"Get her away from here," he said to

Younger. "Cut around them and head for Hawthorn. That's the only place she'll be half safe tonight. I'll try to pull them off until you can get a start."

He didn't wait for an answer. He put the grey into motion, heading down the lane for the road.

Behind him, Younger laughed as he helped Myra into the saddle. "You should have stuck with him, honey. Believe me, I'll never run my neck into a noose, just to make sure you're safe."

Shamus wasted no worry on himself. The grey was tired, but so were the horses ridden by Burton's men. The grey should be able to outrun them all.

The important thing now was to attract attention to himself so Myra Dodge could reach the canyon safely. She had lost the fight. Her ranch buildings were gone. He doubted if Younger could hold the crew together, and now, with Burton's ranch burned, the Bar X would hunt the valley for her. But if she could get to Hawthorn tonight she would be all right until he could get there and take her through the tunnel, out of the valley.

He pulled the rifle from its boot, bringing it up to rest across the saddle horn, and sat quietly, waiting.

The first riders came into sight. He fired over their heads. He couldn't hit anything at that range, but he had no desire to kill any of them.

They hauled up, spreading out quickly. He fired twice, then sent the horse along the road, headed for Belmont. Behind him a dozen rifles blossomed in the darkness, and voices cried out his name.

Now he would be blamed for burning the ranch. All up and down the valley people would call him an outlaw.

He rode on for two miles, then slacked his pace to listen. The sounds of pursuit were fainter now, but still coming on. He smiled grimly, patting the arched neck of the sweating grey.

Well, he had wanted them to follow him, hadn't he?

He kept to the easy pace until they sighted him, and spurring ahead for another four miles. He judged that they had come far enough on the road. It was no part of his plan to enter Belmont, or to be on the road when daylight came. He pulled off on a rocky shoulder above the next creek and angled into the brush which clothed its banks.

He was a quarter of a mile from the highway when Burton's riders thundered past. He listened, judging that there might be ten of them, and frowned, wondering where the others were, wondering whether Myra Dodge and Younger had made good their escape.

Then he dismounted, walking for a mile, giving the grey a chance to blow. Again he swung into the saddle, cutting across the valley toward the hollow where the stock had been bedded near Cow Creek.

Three times during the night he heard other riders. Each time he sought cover, standing with his hand across the grey's nose, ready to squeeze the nostrils if the horse showed signs of wanting to nicker.

He did not know whether these riders were part of Burton's crew out combing the valley floor, or Hawthorn men, scattering as they fled from the Bar X, but he took no chance.

At daybreak he was still a full three miles from the bed grounds. He pushed on quickly, expecting to hear cattle stirring. He heard nothing.

As nearly as he could estimate, yesterday's gather ran between six and seven hundred head, and his puzzlement grew as he mounted the last rise and looked down on a meadow-like bend in the creek.

This was the bed ground, all right. The

flattened grass and broken bushes bore mute testimony. But the cattle were gone and so were the men who should have been guarding them.

He took the grey around the trampled ground, studying sign. Part of the herd had been driven northward. He could not tell how many, although he followed the tracks for several hundred yards.

He turned back, covering the bed ground again, picking out other trails. These led directly into the hills and his puzzlement grew. He followed the plainest of the sign. It led him over a hogback, down into a small canyon and then north, sticking to the timber.

Having nothing better to do, he followed this trail. At ten o'clock he climbed out of another canyon and saw the cattle. Four men were pushing them through the brush, taking it easy-like. He got within two hundred feet before they noticed him.

They stopped, spreading a little as he rode up. They acted wary, watching his every move. He nodded and sat tiredly in the saddle, his hands crossed on the high horn. "Where you headed?"

They exchanged glances. They didn't seem to know what to tell him. Finally a black-haired giant said gruffly, "Younger's orders. We're supposed to get them out of sight."

"A good idea. Burton will be looking for them sooner or later."

The black-haired man grinned. "Burton will be some busy the next few days looking for his own cows. The boys have drifted as many of them as they could into the hills and scattered them."

Shamus did not change expression. "Where are you taking these?"

The man hesitated. "To the canyon."

Shamus' surprise grew. The sparse grass on the floor and steep slopes of the canyon would not support the cows for long, and he wondered what Younger was trying to pull. But this hardly seemed to be the time or the place to find out.

He borrowed some food from the four men and ate for the first time in twenty hours. When he left them, they were still working the cattle slowly northward. At four that afternoon he cut into the trail just before it made its bend into the canyon mouth.

He rode with caution, but not expecting trouble. When the rifle spoke, high on the right canyon wall, it startled him. He reigned in thinking Burton's crew must have gotten here before him and set up an ambush.

But there was no cover, no place to hide. The only brush in sight was the scrub along the river below him and the trees which clung to the rocks above. He sat still, holding the reins in one hand, holding his other up in a sign of peace, and scanned the wall of the canyon. Finally, through the fence of tree trunks, he saw movement in a rock pile a hundred feet up.

"What's the matter?" he called.

The man got to his feet, holding his rifle ready. At that distance Shamus could not recognize the bearded face.

"No one goes up the canyon, Magee. Younger's orders."

"But hell, I'm on your side."

"You especially," the man called. "Younger said you weren't to pass. Get moving." As if to punctuate his words he raised the rifle and laid a shot into the trail twenty feet in front of Shamus.

The grey horse shied and he swung it around. The fool, he thought. The fool. Younger was boxing himself and his crew and the Diamond D cattle in the canyon. They could hold it for a spell, but sooner or later Burton would dig them out.

17

Long before noon, Tim Younger led Myra Dodge through the drainage tunnel into Pine Canyon. He had blindfolded two horses and brought the nervous animals safely through to the other side. There they mounted and rode for the railroad construction camp.

In Younger's mind a plan had been forming all night, a plan to cheat Dr. Clare out of his share of the money for the stolen cattle.

To start with, he meant to approach the ex-sutler, Sorrel, tell him that Myra Dodge was the owner of the Diamond D, and explain that since they were delivering meat from lawful cattle the full price should go to her.

They rode into the camp shortly after one o'clock, and the first man Younger saw when he entered the commisary was Clare. He stopped, staring at the doctor as at a ghost, and indeed Clare looked more nearly dead than alive.

"What are you doing here, Doc?"

The doctor made no effort to stand up. His lips were colorless, his face grey. "They sent for me last night. Marty got away."

"Got away?"

"She bribed one of the China boys with that ruby ring she had. She was gone when Florence went to feed her this morning."

Younger sat down slowly, thankful that he had left Myra outside. "Where would she go?"

"Probably to hunt Magee. She wouldn't go back to Belmont — not until she's had a chance to tell Magee about the tunnel."

"I'll find her."

Clare tried to rise then, but the pain was worse, much worse, and the long ride up here had sapped his fast failing strength. "You won't hurt her?"

"Of course not." Younger was already on his feet.

"If you do I'll tell the full story to the authorities."

"Why should I hurt her?" Younger said. "I'm not a fool. We're in this together, aren't we?"

He wasted no more time on the doctor. He went outside and told Myra Dodge what had happened.

"You'll have to stay here until I find her," he said. "If she blabs about the tunnel the whole thing is finished and we're trapped in that canyon with those cattle."

"But how will you find her?"

He grinned. "You know that crazy song

Magee made up? The one he sings all the time?"

She nodded.

"She'll be in the hills, looking for Magee. Maybe she rode down to your ranch and found it burned. If so, she'd go back to the hills, figuring that's where he'd be."

"Well?"

"I'll let her find me," Younger said. "I'll ride through there tonight, following the main trails, singing that song. I can't sing, but neither can Magee. She'll hear me and show herself."

Myra frowned doubtfully. "And if you do find her?"

"I'll see she doesn't talk."

"And what will the doctor do then?"

"He won't do anything. He's dying. I've known it for weeks. He had to tell someone. But I didn't think it would come so fast. Take a look at him through the window."

She looked.

"If he doesn't die fast enough," Younger said, "I can help him. Now, I'm going to take you in and introduce you to Mrs. Sorrell. You can tell her who you are. Tell her you're going to stay here to check on the meat deliveries . . ."

Tim Younger had prowled the country for

weeks, trying to familiarize himself with all the twisting trails of these hills. He did not know which one Marty Clare would take, but as he rode away from the railroad camp he tried to follow her mind, to figure out what she would do in terms of her own logic.

She would stay toward the north, and low down in the ragged foothills from which in daylight she could watch the sweep of the valley floor. And she would stay near water. That narrowed it a lot. He remembered a dozen spots in which she might have camped.

Sometime after midnight he came off the military ridge and dropped eastward down a winding canyon. The moon was a crescent, hanging high and pale, but it gave him enough light to see the bare line of the deer trail he followed, and as soon as he had left the higher timberland he began to sing.

He could not recall more than two verses of the song, and he knew he was doing it badly, but it would serve his purpose if the girl heard him. Her camp would be well hidden, but if he covered enough territory she might come to him.

He kept to the trail, until it dropped below timber and was lost in the grassland below. Then he turned northward, finding another canyon and angling up it until he reached the two-thousand-foot level.

He had little fear of running into Burton's men this far north. He might hit some of the boys from Hawthorn who were scattered in the hills, still working the Diamond D stock toward the canyon, but he guessed they would stay hidden even if they heard him.

Four hours later he was ready to give up. He halted the horse beside a small creek, allowing it to drink, and considered the situation. After daybreak, which was less than half an hour away, his ruse would not work. Marty could recognize him in the light. The thing to do, he decided, was to round up as many Hawthorn men as he could and comb the hills for the girl. He headed his horse back up the canyon, beginning the verse again more from habit than hope.

And then her voice reached him from the hillside.

"Shamus! Shamus Magee!"

He reined in, pulling his hat brim lower, although she should not be able to recognize him in the deep shadow of the canyon bottom.

"Shamus, it's Marty."

"Yeah." It was more a grunt than a word. He could not trust his speaking voice to fool her. He heard crackling above him as she slid down through the brush. He waited. She came down beside him and he dropped from his horse.

"Younger!" She whirled, but his left hand snaked out to catch her arm.

"Easy, kid."

She tried to fight free. She was not wearing her little gun. They had taken it from her at the railroad camp. She twisted and turned in his grasp, kicking at his shins with her small boots.

He cuffed her across the mouth with the back of his hand. A little blood appeared on her lower lip where it had been cut against her teeth.

"What are you going to do with me?" she panted.

He eased his hold slightly. "That depends on how much sense you have."

"If you mean will I keep quiet about your tunnel the answer is no."

He said, "You're a fool. Your father's in this as deep as I am."

"I know it." The admission hurt her worse than the bite of his fingers.

In the quickening morning light Younger's face was wolfish. "Don't make any mistake, kiddo. Don't get the idea that your being a woman will make a difference to me. I've killed people before this to get what I want, and I can do it again."

She tensed her body, knowing he told the truth, knowing she might not leave this canyon alive. And then from the trees above them a voice she recognized said quietly:

"Let her go, Younger — and keep your hand away from that gun."

Tim Younger also knew the voice. He let his hands fall away from the girl and stood stiffly as Shamus Magee came out of the trees and slid to the canyon floor.

The sun was not yet up, but the broadening band of light in the east cast the world around them in eerie, grey shadow.

Younger's lips were numb as he asked, "How'd you happen to show up?"

"I didn't happen to. I've been trailing you half the night."

Younger's face broke with consternation. Shamus said, "You didn't think you could ride around these hills singing my song without my wondering what you were up to?"

Younger cursed himself under his breath. He had thought of the possibility of running into Burton's men, of perhaps being seen or heard by riders from Hawthorn, but for some reason it had not occurred to him that Magee would pick up his trail.

"I was camped under the ridge when you rode by," Shamus said. "I couldn't figure who was singing, so I followed. The more you sashayed back and forth the more I was sure you were after something. But I didn't think it was Marty."

"Now listen." Younger had recovered and his brain was busy. "I meant her no harm. I was just getting a message to her about her father. He's sick."

"Sick?"

The girl said quickly, "It's a trick. He's trying to cover up, Shamus. He's trying to make me keep quiet about the tunnel."

"Tunnel?" A picture of her as he had seen her at the old mine leaped into his head. "What about the tunnel, Marty?"

"They're going to use it. He and my father are stealing cattle. They intend to butcher them at the mine and carry the meat through the mountain to Pine Valley and haul it to the railroad camps."

Shamus whistled between his teeth. Many things which had puzzled him were falling into place. "So that's it."

"I overheard them talking. I told my father. He took me up to the railroad camp and left me there, a prisoner. I got away and came looking for you."

Shamus felt bleak. He said, "Maybe you'd

better talk a little yourself, Younger. Did Myra Dodge know about this?"

Younger hesitated, wondering how much to tell Magee, wondering what would profit him most. He nodded. "She knew."

"That you were planning to steal her cattle?"

"That's right."

"And rustle some of Burton's?"

"Maybe."

"I've been a prize sucker, haven't I?"

Younger didn't answer.

"I should kill you," Shamus said. "Another man probably would, for double-crossing him, for what you tried to do to Marty. Give me your gun."

Younger drew his gun. He made no effort to swing it on Magee. He handed it over, butt first.

Shamus backed to Younger's horse. He pulled the rifle from the boot and flung it into the bushes. "All right. Ride out. If I see you in this country again I'll kill you."

Marty opened her mouth to protest. Shamus saw and motioned with his head. In silence they watched Younger mount and ride down the canyon.

"You shouldn't have let him go." The words burst from the girl. "The hills are alive with Hawthorn men. I saw them yesterday."

He shrugged tiredly. "What was I supposed to do, kill him? We couldn't hold him prisoner. We couldn't take him with us because we have no place to go. Burton is after me. So are most of the bush jumpers, I suppose. I've made a wonderful mess of things."

"No, Shamus. It wasn't your fault."

"Wasn't it?" he said bitterly. "You tried to warn me about the Dodge woman. You said I was being used, and I wouldn't listen."

"Oh, Shamus." Suddenly she was in his arms, clinging tightly to his shoulders with her small hands. "I'm scared. I'm scared"

He had never seen her thus before. He held her tight, and without thought he lowered his head and kissed her gently. It seemed a good and natural thing. When he started to draw away again she held him as if her very life depended on it.

"Shamus."

"Yes?"

"I know you think I'm a silly child, that I've made your life miserable, but I didn't know how else to get you to notice me."

He smiled in spite of his worry.

"And now I don't know what to do and I haven't anyone else to turn to. What should

I do about my father?"

He looked down into her grey green eyes, reading the desperation there. "I don't know, Marty."

"I should go to the sheriff. I should go to Burton and tell them all about it. That would clear you, wouldn't it? That would make them leave you alone?"

He hesitated. "The sheriff might listen." He doubted if Burton would. Too much had built up between him and the big rancher to be easily forgotten. The only way he saw to avoid trouble was to ride over the hill, to put as many miles as possible between himself and this valley. Once he had considered it a wonderful place to live. Now it had turned into a sort of hell.

He said, "I can't tell you what to do. What did Younger mean by saying that your father was sick?"

"He hasn't been well — I know that — but he's never complained. I think Younger was just trying to play on my feelings, to keep me from telling you about the tunnel."

He frowned at thought of the tunnel. The information should certainly be turned over to the sheriff, but there were other considerations — Marty's father, and the men around Hawthorn. He did not doubt that they had fallen in whole-heartedly with

Younger's plans, but after all it was he, Shamus Magee, who had recruited them for the Diamond D in the first place.

This brought Myra Dodge back to mind, and he wondered now if there had been truth in the story of the stolen bill of sale, truth in the rest of the stories Cole had told Marty. He squirmed inwardly. No man likes to be made a fool, especially by a woman.

But his first job was to get Marty out of the hills safely. He had Younger's guns, but if Younger made connections with some of the Hawthorn men he might come back for more trouble.

He said, "We'd better ride. Your horse above?"

She nodded. He picked up Younger's rifle and sixgun and handed them to Marty. They reached the spot where she had picketed her horse, then moved on to the grey.

He said, "The problem is to get you back to Belmont. You'll be safe enough there, but I can't ride in with you. I might meet the sheriff. And I can't leave you alone because of Younger."

She sat quietly in the saddle, watching him with wide eyes. He had never seen her so subdued.

"Whatever shall I do?" she said. "I can't tell the sheriff about Doc. I simply can't,

Shamus. Do you think I'm weak?"

He said, "I think you're wonderful," and with a slow kind of surprise knew that he meant it. She was just about the most wonderful person he had ever known.

"But they've got to be stopped, Shamus. We can't just sit by while they steal all the cattle in the valley."

"There's another way."

"How?"

"If I closed that tunnel they couldn't get rid of the meat."

She drew her breath sharply.

"A little dynamite would fix it so no one could ever get it reopened."

"But then — then all those men would be trapped up there for Burton to butcher at his leisure."

"They can get out on foot. There are trails over the ridge. There's nothing you can take a horse over, but a man can make it easy, walking and climbing."

"Then we *can* stop them. No one need ever know my father was mixed up in it. Shamus, thank you." All her old enthusiasm rushed back into her voice. "Why didn't I think of that when I discovered the tunnel, instead of just telling Doc I knew what he was up to? Come on, let's go!"

"Where?"

"Up to Pine Canyon, of course."

"Where are we going to get the dynamite, Marty? You don't happen to have a dozen sticks in your pocket, do you?"

Her face fell. "Shamus, I'm a dunce, and I always figured I was so smart. You must have a terrible time with me."

"I'm not wise myself," he said absently, wrinkling his brow, remembering something. "Let's call it even — and don't worry, I just remembered where there is some dynamite. I saw a couple of cases at Crowley's store."

"In Hawthorn?" She shook her head anxiously. "You can't get up into the canyon if they're guarding it, and if you did get in there Younger would have you killed."

"I'll take a wee bit of killing," he reminded her. "As for getting in, why can't I go through the tunnel?"

"The tunnel, yes. Come on."

"You're not coming with me."

"I certainly am! You think I'd let you go alone, when you're doing this to save Doc?"

He looked at her helplessly. She complicated things so damn much.

"You'd better go to your father, Marty."

"Why?"

"Younger said he was sick. Don't you

think you ought to go into Belmont and find out?"

"Younger just said that to scare me."

"Maybe. I hope so. But I got the feeling that he meant it, that he wasn't lying."

She frowned, worrying the idea around in her small head.

"So the smart thing is for me to ride down with you to the edge of timber," Shamus said. "Once you're out on the valley floor I think you'll be safe. Burton's men won't touch you, and Younger and the Hawthorn bunch aren't likely to show themselves out of the hills in daytime."

"I'm going with you, Shamus."

He said brutally, "You're a spoiled brat. I thought maybe you'd learned some sense in the last few days. I see you haven't. You want help, all right. But for once in your life do what I tell you. If you don't, I want no more to do with you."

She stared down at him and he was afraid she was going to cry. Without another word he turned and swung into the grey's saddle and led the way southeast through the hills. He did not look back. He rode stiffly, and the clink of her horse's shoes on the loose rocks told him that she was following him.

18

They traveled in silence for a full hour, working downward cautiously, pausing to examine every draw before they dropped into it.

He had no desire to run into Younger or the Hawthorn riders. All he wanted at the time was to get Marty safely down into the rolling grassland.

Closer to it, he rode with less care, certain that they had left the danger from the mountain men well behind — and so it was that he came around a sharp bend in a small canyon and found himself in plain view of a dozen riders.

He jerked his horse to a halt and Marty almost ran into him. They were fully three hundred yards below him but he recognized Bud Cole's long form even before he heard the shout from the Bar X foreman.

"There he is!"

One of the riders behind Cole snapped a trigger-happy shot from his forty-five. The slug went wild, striking the canyon wall to the right of Shamus. But the sound of the shot broke the tableau which had held them all poised like statues for a long, breathless moment.

Shamus swung the grey around, bumping

Marty's horse, almost knocking her from her seat in his effort to shield her.

"Back, Marty. Up the canyon."

Marty Clare had spent most of her waking life in the saddle. She pulled the frightened horse under quick control, swinging it and charging up the canyon. Shamus pulled aside to let her pass and then rode after her.

The curve they had rounded just before they saw the Bar X men acted as bulwark, and by the time Bud Cole led his crew around it Shamus and Marty had reached and turned into a side draw, scrambling upward toward the shelter of the timber.

At the top of the draw they crested a small hogback and followed it, only to run into a burst of rocks. They could not pass the rocks and had to swing left, down the steep bank into the floor of a second canyon.

Up this they hurried. There was no trail and the pole pine grew so thick that they had difficulty in forcing a passage. Behind them, made faint by the screen of trees and upthrusts of the bordering rock, they could hear the muffled shouts of their pursuers.

Shamus pulled up beside Marty, motioning for her to halt. "Cut downhill," he said. "They won't expect me to go that way. They know I don't dare let them crowd me out into the valley. Cut down and ride for

Belmont. You'll be all right."

She shook her head, but he wasted no time in further argument. He reached over, slapping her nervous horse, and saw the animal bear away, down-canyon. For himself he headed straight across, the grey snorting as its hoofs dug hard for footing in the thin soil.

They made it somehow, although the wall was so steep that Shamus doubted whether he could have climbed it on foot, and topped out between two upthrusts of granite each larger than a good-sized building.

He pulled up, letting the quivering horse blow, listening to the sounds in the timber below him. He wanted them to follow him long enough to let Marty get away.

For this purpose he fired two shots into the trees, then rode along the crest of the hill until he found another canyon, leading again toward the high rim. The country was extremely rough and he could make better time than his pursuers because they must pause to search out his tracks. On the other hand, he ran the chance of reaching a point past which he could not climb, and being forced back down the hill.

He glanced at the sky, judging that it was not yet midday, and wished fervently for darkness. Night would give him a chance to circle back to one of the trails that led over the top. He climbed, and a new danger faced him, for now he was not far below timberline. Above it the snowfields glistened white, soft snow, in spots at least ten feet deep under the slanting rays of the summer sun.

They could not be crossed safely, so he angled north, bringing up suddenly on the brink of a deep canyon.

He stared downward, noting the loose rubble which, freed by the frost, had tumbled down the almost vertical bank, lodging here and there against a tree trunk or rocky upthrust. He might be able to make it to the bottom without his horse, but he could not hope to get the grey down this face.

He turned, riding upward along its edge, forced to detour by the broken ground and deep side washes which cut into it on the south. After half an hour he realized that he had been riding in a huge circle. He was now above but not much more than a mile from the spot where he and Marty had separated.

For the first time since this flight had started, he knew a sense of panic. He did not underestimate Bud Cole and the Bar X crew. They knew these hills better than he did, and they would keep coming until they dropped, because to their way of thinking the burning of the Bar X was as great a crime as could be committed. Some would hang on his trail grimly, and some would have spread out to prevent him from drifting around them.

He sat listening. Above him the timber thinned, the trees no longer grew straight, pointing to the distant sky, but were twisted and bent, misshapen by the almost constant wind which swept the long bare stretches above timberline.

There was something stark and desolate and lonely about the higher hills. Even the wind sounded threatening and hostile and he shivered a little as he nudged his horse downward, hoping in the deeper timber to find some spot where he could conceal the grey, where he could wait until night gave him a chance to slip the tightening noose.

He rode silently, carefully, pausing every few feet to listen, his path taking him down a hogback whose rocky soil would leave small sign for searching eyes.

After another quarter of a mile he came on a deer trail leading upward. He took his time studying it. A deer can travel ground which a horse cannot, but the fact that the well-worn track lifted toward the summit might mean that there was a pass above. If so, he might get the grey over the high ridge to the west side of the mountains.

He kneed the grey into the trail. The timber pressed so closely on each side of the trace that in places the horse had all it could do to force a passage. They dipped into a shallow wash and climbed again, and then the trail turned, running along the rocky rim of a deep canyon.

He was afraid that at any moment the trail might go over the canyon wall, and downward to the small stream far below. Instead, it continued to climb, the trees thining now so that he had occasional glimpses of the snow above.

And then the track bent away from the canyon, around a burst of jutting rock which rose forty feet into the air. He circled the rock burst. The trail started back to the canyon rim, and then without warning a man seemed to drop from the sky, landing on the grey behind him. An arm circled his neck, a gun pressed into his side, and Bud Cole's voice said, "I figured you'd use this track."

Shamus halted the grey. He sat motionless in the saddle, the pressure of Cole's arm about his throat not quite choking him.

"You're not very smart, Magee. You

thought we'd trail you, hunt you through the timber. You were wrong. We figured you had to get on the ridge, and to do that there are only five trails. We sent men up to cover them all."

Shamus sat very still.

"I'm going to slide off now," Cole said. "I could have shot you out of the saddle, but I wanted you alive. Burton will enjoy hanging you himself, Magee."

He released his hold. "Don't try anything or I'll gutshoot you." He was on the ground in an instant, his extremely long legs making the movement easy.

"All right, Magee. Get down."

Shamus flipped a leg over the saddle and sat sidewise. Had the trail been wider and less steep he would have tried spurring the grey ahead, chancing a shot, knowing he had little or nothing to lose. But on this steeply slanting track he had no hope of escape that way. He sat for a moment, resting, thinking. He slid down the horse's side, appearing to stumble as he did so. He fell forward, and one hand hit Cole's gun hand, knocking it aside.

The gun exploded. The bullet struck the grey in the neck. The stallion screamed and reared, but Shamus did not even see it. His arms were locked about Cole's body as he tried to carry the tall man to the ground.

Cole's gun clattered on the rocks and his arms closed around Shamus' neck. They went down, rolling over and over on the rough ground, coming up with a jarring thud against the bole of a tree. The back of Shamus' neck struck the tree so hard that it numbed him and he lost his grip. Bud Cole tore free.

He scrambled backward on hands and knees like a land crab trying to escape. But he was after the fallen gun, and he had it almost in his grasp when Shamus grabbed his shoulder and hauled him away.

Again Cole broke free. This time he rolled, coming to his feet. There was a line of blood across his lean cheek where a sharp rock had cut it. Shamus could see the blood and even as he rose he drove his right fist toward it.

Cole stepped inside, letting the right slide across his shoulder as he ducked, and driving his fist into Shamus' ribs with enough force to stop him for an instant. Then Shamus seemed to explode. He swarmed over the taller man, no longer trying for the head, but driving short blows into the body with both hands.

Cole gave ground, backing around the rock pile, trying to block the blows and at the same time wrap his arms around Shamus. But Shamus was as hard to hold as a buzzsaw. He kept boring in, his head down, a cut above one eye leaking blood which half blinded him.

They were both too groggy to realize how near the canyon rim they had come, and they circled the rock burst until they stood on the very edge.

Shamus could have been the one who went over, but it did not happen that way. The rock onto which Cole backed was loosely bedded. He knew his danger suddenly and tried to bull forward. Shamus' fist caught him squarely in the neck.

He staggered, missed one step, and then a high yell wrenched out of his throat. He fell, arms wide, legs spread, dropping some thirty feet before he smashed sidewise on the edge of a narrow rock ledge. His body rested there an instant and then rolled off to fall clear for a hundred feet to the floor of broken stone below.

Shamus almost went over himself, the force of his blow carrying him forward. He dropped to his knees, staring dumbly into the canyon as Cole's body twisted through the air.

He was so beaten that he stayed thus for a while just dragging tortured air into his battered lungs. At last he backed away from the rim and stood up gingerly, feeling himself all over to be sure that his bones were still in place.

Somewhere in the fight he had lost his gun. He walked back around the rock shoulder, squinting blearily at the ground, searching for the gun. He did not realize that he was not alone until he came all the way around the rock and saw the four riders in the trail beyond the fallen grey.

He turned to run, but it was already too late. A shot chipped rock close to his head and a hoarse voice told him to hold up. He stopped, using his hand limply to wipe the blood from his eyes, and stared half blindly at the Bar X men.

They surrounded him in a moment, grabbing his arms, shaking him.

"Where's Bud Cole?"

He gestured toward the canyon rim.

One of the men walked around the upthrust rock. When he came back he was white under the tanned hardness of his face.

"My God, he threw him over."

Shamus wanted to tell them that he had not thrown Cole over the rim, that it had been an accident in a fair fight. But even as he opened his mouth he knew it was no use. Nothing he said would convince them, would make the least difference.

A stringy, dried-up rider whom he had known for years glared at him. "I guess when a man goes bad, Magee, he goes real bad." He reached out and slapped Shamus across his already battered mouth.

"Damn you, Bud Cole was the best friend I had. One of you get a rope."

There was a man on each side of Magee, holding his arms. He considered it an unnecessary precaution. He was so tired that his hands seemed to be made of lead. He could not have raised them if he tried.

The man with the rope came back. He swiveled his head, examining the trees around him, selecting one with a limb jutting out about twenty feet above the ground. Expertly he flipped the rope end over it and stood fashioning a hangman's knot as if he had never had a job that pleased him more.

"All right," he said, "get him on a horse."

Shamus' guards walked him over to a horse and boosted him into the saddle his hands tied behind him. He felt the rough edge of the rope around his neck and knew that in a matter of seconds he would be dangling free.

He said a small, voiceless prayer. He was not overly religious, but nature had taught him to believe in an authority higher than man. Then he smiled. He wanted it to be a scornful, hang-me-and-be-damned sort of smile. He did the best he could.

19

Mushy Calder had ridden the hills alone since the burning of the ranch. Avarice was not among his faults, and he had no desire to join the groups of Hawthorn men who were rustling the valley cattle and working it into the rough hills.

In fact he had no desire to join anyone. He realized better than most what the burning of the two ranches meant, and while he hated Burton with a slow, festering hate he did not intend to involve himself in a hopeless range war.

But curiosity was his besetting sin. He simply had to know more about what was going on, because Younger's actions puzzled him. So he stayed in the hills rather than cross the divide to the safety of the western slope.

He had trapped the country for forty years, and he knew every trail and hiding place as thoroughly as the average man knows his own yard. He felt little fear of being caught in a box canyon or trapped by some ambush.

He stayed high, and his wolfer's eyes, which could read sign near and far with incredible accuracy, bared every movement of the men below him. He watched them as they rode across bare ground, only to disappear into the heavy timber of the canyons, and he saw the hunt develop as the Bar X moved upward to close in on Magee.

He shifted along the ridge as Magee circled, spotted Burton's men as they emerged above their quarry, and knew that Shamus would ride into the trap.

He argued with himself, saying he was a fool to take any interest, saying he should keep out of it. Not until he heard the shot as Magee grabbed for Cole's gun did he make up his mind, and although he hurried, the rope was already around Magee's neck before he left his horse and slipped on down the dimness of the deer trail.

Mushy Calder came out on a rock shoulder above the necktie party but he did not open fire immediately. If he spooked the horse on which Magee sat, without hitting the right target at the right time, Shamus would be jerked clear to kick his life away. Mushy was a practical man.

He aimed his rifle delicately and drilled the man who held the loose end of the rope. The horse jumped, and with its jump Shamus expected that his neck would snap. Instead, the rope ran free, up across the limb, and the frightened horse was fifty yards up the steep track before it slowed.

Calder wasted no time on sentiment. His second shot dropped the man who had tied the hangman's knot, his third caught another rider in the back as he ran for his horse.

Only one of the Bar X four managed to make his escape, and he did so by ignoring his horse and diving into the shelter of the timber.

But the fight was out of him and he continued downward, his progress marked by the racket he made slipping and sliding over the rocks. He had no idea how many men might have been in the attack, and at the moment he had no urge to learn.

Shamus, with his wrists bound behind him and the knotted rope still trailing from his neck, was nearly helpless. His feet had been purposely left free of the stirrups, and he struggled to find them as Calder glided down the trail to his side.

From the ground he regarded Shamus with cynical amusement. "You look like a turkey, all fixed up for roasting."

"Quit gabbing and cut me loose before they come back."

Calder spat at a rock. "There ain't but one of them to come back."

"There are others in the hills."

"Sure. I've been watching them." Mushy drew a long skinning knife from his belt and slashed the bonds on Shamus' wrists. "I guess you can lift the collar from your own neck."

Shamus could and did. He threw the rope from him with quick distaste. Then he looked at the little wolfer who was grinning sardonically. "If it hadn't been for you I'd have taken my last dance, Mushy. I guess maybe I'll never really enjoy dancing again."

"If you don't get out of this valley you sure won't." Calder handed him his gun, which he had found near the trail. "What are you antigodlin around these hills for, like a partridge ready to be plucked?"

Shamus told him. He told about Younger's plan to rustle the beef, butcher it and haul the meat through the tunnel. Calder's eyes gleamed as he listened. He thoroughly appreciated the subtleties of the plan, and his lawless soul regretted that he had not thought of it. Not that he would have bothered to do anything about it.

Shamus said, "You were asking me what I was doing in the hills. The question goes double."

"Had to know what was going on." Calder spat again. "Now that I know I can pull out. Figure Younger can give Burton all the trouble he needs. That's the only reason I got you into this, to give Burton trouble."

"Thought you were helping the Dodge woman?"

Calder snickered. "Now she's the Dodge woman. Last time I saw you she was sweet and kind and you were making calf eyes."

"A man can make a mistake, damn it."

Calder was cackling now. "Sure you can. I figured she was no-account when I first pulled her out of that cabin. She even tried her flimflams on me, and a woman that will look twice at a man like me either's got a purpose of her own or a head full of rocks. But you was a natural."

"I should bust you, Mushy."

Calder said slowly, "You know, you should at that," and he said it in a tone Shamus had never heard him use. "You're a good guy, Shamus. You treated me decenter than anyone ever has, and I done you a lot of dirt. Maybe that's why I hung around, maybe that's why I come busting down when they were about to hang you. I never had a partner like you." He broke off as if ashamed of his unnatural softness, and his tone changed.

"Damn you, Shamus. People like you shouldn't run around making muscles. You can act tough, and fight tough, but you ain't tough underneath. You got to be pushed or tricked into a fracas. You don't get no pleasure out of killing. I'll bet right this minute you're fretting because Cole went off that rim."

Shamus had nothing to say.

"Well, don't give him a thought. He'd have thrown you off if he could. That's what I mean. You ain't cold, mean, on-purpose tough enough to fight for long and go on living. You think a full minute before you level on a man and pull the trigger — and believe me, the other man don't. He'll kill you while you're thinking about it."

Shamus stared at him. "By golly, I never heard you talk like that before."

Calder's mouth twisted cynically. "I wasn't always a wolfer. Forget it. Come on, we'll ride over the ridge and leave this damn country."

"I have to do something first."

"What?"

"Blow that tunnel so Younger can't steal any more beef."

"In the name of heaven why is it your business?"

"Well, I started this and I've got to stop

it." He did not add that Marty's father was involved, and he had to stop it so she wouldn't feel obliged to go to the sheriff with what she knew.

"You didn't start it, Shamus. I did. I put the bee in Myra Dodge's bonnet to fight Burton — not that she wasn't spoiling to do it. I suckered you into the play, and into riding to Hawthorn, and I'm not worrying about blowing any tunnel. To hell with it. Let Burton stomp his own snakes, and let him get killed a-stomping. Come on, let's ride before them other Bar X hands get here and we have to shoot the lot of them."

They rode, Calder in the lead, following the deer trail upward until it was lost on the rocky ground near the edge of the snow-bank. Mushy rode steadily, sure of himself, and Shamus tailed him. The Bar X horse he had taken was no match for the dead grey, but it was a solid animal and seemed fairly fresh.

Mushy Calder never hesitated. He skirted the drifts, studying the ground above as he progressed, and finally waded his horse into the snow. The stuff came above the horses' knees, slowing them to a creeping walk, but never reached a depth through which they could not flounder. At last they came to a notch in the rock wall and started down the western slope.

Once out of the snow and back into the timber, Calder wanted to continue west, but Shamus hauled up. "Can't do it, Mushy. I've got things to attend to."

Calder cursed him roundly. "Where you going to get the dynamite? You can't go near Belmont. Maybe you could talk a foreman out of some at the railroad camps, but I doubt it, especially if that commissary is in on the stealing."

"There's some at Crowley's store."

Calder groaned. "You mean you're going into that canyon? You're a worse fool than I even thought you were, and that's saying a good deal. Why, there's fifty men in there would cut your throat in a minute if they knew what you were up to. How you going to get inside the canyon anyhow?"

"Through the tunnel."

Calder spat. "I give up. I know you. You're too hard-headed to argue with. Why I didn't let the Bar X hang you and be done with it I'll never know. Well, so long."

"So long."

"Keep down this creek for about a mile. There's a break in the canyon wall, an old rock slide with a deer trail. Follow that. It'll bring you down into Pine Valley, save you eight or ten miles."

He turned without another word and rode westward.

Shamus watched him go, feeling very much alone. Then he swung the horse to the right and followed the creek down grade. It was nearly sundown when he rode to the head of Pine Valley. He dismounted, hobbled the horse in a small grassy meadow which ran down to a side stream, and began to climb toward the tunnel's mouth.

He found fresh tracks up the mountain and guessed that these had been made by wagons from the grading camps carrying away the stolen meat. This meant Younger's men were already in business, and he approached the tunnel with renewed caution. But there was no sign of anyone around the entrance, no light showing within.

He had no lamp and he would not have used it if he had one. He dreaded stumbling again through the heavy darkness of the mountain's heart, but there was no other way. He paused, taking a last look at the valley he was leaving.

The sun had gone, and shadows stretched from one side of the valley to the other. It would be dark before he reached the mill buildings of the old mine.

The passage seemed shorter this time. For one thing, he knew how far he had to travel.

He groped his way along, feeling the slimy wetness of the rock walls and the timbers as he passed, deciding that whatever he did in the future, if he had one, it would not involve working underground.

It was night outside so he could not see the end of the tunnel as he approached it, but he sensed the change in the air and moved forward stealthily, his gun ready in his hand.

The old tunnel house was dark and deserted, but the mill buildings below showed light. He crept down the shoulder of the dump and peered through a crack. He saw a dozen cattle carcasses hanging, and men in bloody aprons cutting up more animals on an improvised wooden block.

It seemed to him the meat would be tough and stringy, not having been properly hung, but he supposed the Irishmen in the grading camps would offer no complaint.

Noting that Younger was not present, Shamus wondered whether he had made his way back into the canyon or was still outside. Then he turned and slid down the dump to the street below.

He moved with caution, but took comfort in the number of people about. Nobody would pay much attention to him unless they saw his face in clear light. The canyon was like a fort, with plenty of watchers guarding the lower entrance, so the people here felt safe from the attack by Burton's men. He had been surprised to find the tunnel unguarded, but that could mean either that Younger had resumed his efforts to catch and silence Marty, or did not believe she would open her mouth for fear of involving her father. Or . . . well, he just couldn't figure it out.

He waited his chance and ducked behind the crumbling row of old buildings. He dared not approach Crowley's store this early. The place would be filled with people. He would have to wait until the town settled down for the night.

He found a place on the hillside behind the former saloon and sat down, realizing suddenly how bone tired he was. It seemed to him that it had been months since he had slept. He dozed.

20

Cold awakened him and he stretched, not recalling where he was. Then abruptly he was alert. The store below him was dark. Nothing moved along the street.

He stood up, cursing himself softly. If he had slept too long, he would have had to hide through a whole day. He had no watch, but the feel of morning was in the air even though the canyon rim opposite hid any chance of seeing lighter sky.

He slid down the steep bank and stepped behind the store building. He hated to roust Crowley out, but he knew from past experience that the bearded man was an extremely light sleeper. It would be wise to wake the fat man and explain a few things. Else Crowley might think he heard burglars, and maybe fire a gun and rouse the town. He went to the rear door and knocked.

Crowley unbolted the door. He wore a striped nightshirt of cotton flannel over which his black beard fell like ragged brush. Sleep rimmed his eyes with red and he blinked dully at Shamus. Then recognition came, with a kind of shock.

"What are you doing here, Magee? How'd you get into the canyon past the guards?"

"Tunnel."

It took a while for the fat man to digest this information and what it might mean. "Lucky for you Younger isn't around."

That explained the lack of guards at the tunnel. Partly.

"He gave orders to shoot you on sight," Crowley said. "You'd better get back through that tunnel while your hide is still in one piece."

Shamus pushed his way into the kitchen and closed the door. "For a man who didn't want any trouble with Burton you're right in the middle of things, mister."

Crowley was aggrieved. "And whose fault is it that any of this started? Yours. You're a fine one to be talking to me. What could I do? Either I played their game or they shot me and took over the place."

"You wouldn't be getting any of the money from the stolen meat, I suppose."

Crowley tried to stare him down and failed. His eyes strayed to the floor and he gazed at his swollen, mottled bare feet. "I ain't saying yes, and I ain't saying no, Magee. A man's gotta live. Besides, Burton can't get inside the canyon. There's not a damn thing he can do to stop us."

"You're a fool," Shamus said. "Sooner or later this country will be crawling with U.S. marshals. The sheriff will see to that if Burton doesn't. Younger will grab the money and ride out. The rest of the boys will fade into the brush. What happens to you then? You're stuck here. You've got this store."

From the unhappy quiver of Crowley's jowls, he knew his words were striking home.

"I'm here to give you a chance to help,

Crowley. I'll see that Burton and the sheriff hear that you were the one to stop the stock being carted to the railroad."

Crowley shook his head. "We can't stop them. There's only two of us, and they've gone crazy. They think they'll all be millionaires. You should see them. They're worse than if they was drunk. Younger has really sold them."

"That doesn't matter. I'll stop them."

"How?"

"By blowing the tunnel. If the tunnel is closed they can't get the meat out of the canyon."

The fat man gaped at him in growing horror. "Blow the tunnel? No you don't. How do you think I'll ever get the mine to working again if you block the drainage tunnel?"

Shamus felt sorry for Crowley. The gutted, abandoned old mine would never work again, but nothing he could say would persuade the storekeeper.

"I've got to do it, Crowley. It's the only way."

The fat man cursed him savagely. Then, clumsy-quick, he made a lunge at the gun which lay on the kitchen table. Shamus grabbed him. Crowley was big, but his body was flabby. Shamus pushed rather than hit him. Crowley lumbered across toward the bedroom door. Shamus went after him, drawing his gun. "Don't make me shoot you, Ed." He had no intention of shooting. He did not want to kill Crowley, and a shot would rouse the town. But Crowley did not think of this. He was almost past thinking. His horror at the prospect of destruction in the mine clouded all else.

He turned to fight, like a cornered animal, and Shamus heaved him over onto the tumbled bed, tearing one of the light cotton blankets into strips, binding the swollen ankles, then the wrists.

Crowley pleaded, half weeping, until Shamus forced the gag between his lips. Then he lay there heaving, tears running down to lose themselves in the forest of the beard.

Shamus went into the store room, straight to the corner where he had seen the boxes of dynamite. He hefted one, then caught up a coil of fuse on one hand. Thus burdened he crossed the kitchen and stepped through the rear door.

Greyness had come to the world while he was in the store, softening the darkness, bringing the outlines of the old buildings and the rising canyon wall into sharp relief. He moved quickly along the alley which ran behind the buildings at the foot of the canyon wall. When he reached the upper end of the moldering town, he slipped around the last building and stopped for an instant to reassure himself that the main street was empty.

Hawthorn slept. There was no activity anywhere, not even in the mill buildings which were being used as a slaughterhouse.

Below, in the pens which had been constructed with timbers torn from some of the buildings, the stolen cattle bawled for water, unaware of the fate which awaited them.

Shamus climbed the dump. His plan was simple. All he had to do was walk through the tunnel, thus escaping from the canyon, plant his dynamite at the far end, and light the fuse. The passage would be blocked past the point where it could be cleared in time to do the rustlers any good.

He came into the enginehouse, finding it still dark. He made for the tunnel, and stumbled over an old shaft. He caught the dynamite before it fell, but dropped the fuse. He fumbled until he found it, and then, deciding that he must have a light, he left the box and fuse and slid down to the mill.

Inside, the place reeked of blood from the slaughtered animals. He lit a match, seeing that three carcasses still hung from the rafters, and found what he wanted, a lantern suspended from a nail in one of the beams. He took it down and lighted it, and carried it back up the dump to the enginehouse.

Here he broke open the dynamite box and pulled out the yellow sticks one by one. Next he shook out the sawdust packing and replaced the sticks, tying them together into a bundle, digging a hole in the center of one of them and inserting the cap which he had bitten onto the fuse.

That done, he stuffed the packing back into the box's empty end. But suddenly he heard a sound deep within the tunnel — the rattle of a loose stone as a boot struck it.

He bent quickly, picked up the box with its coil of fuse, and moved it to the side of the tunnel entrance so whoever was coming out would not stumble over it. Then he blew out the lantern and drew his gun, waiting in the half darkness which was now broken by the growing morning light filtering through the chinks in the old walls.

The sound from the tunnel was plainer now and he saw a small light, far away in the well of darkness. It came on. The fellow in there was wearing the light on his hat, so it did not show the shadow of his face.

Shamus waited and waited. As far as he

could trust his ears, there was only one person in the tunnel, and he breathed deeply to ease the tension of his waiting.

And then she stepped out of the tunnel and a cry came out of him. "Marty!"

She stopped, and her small hand dropped instinctively to the gun at her side. Then she saw him in the glow of her tiny light.

"Shamus."

She was in his arms, holding him tightly, sobbing against the firmness of his shoulder.

"Shamus, you're all right."

"Marty, honey, what are you doing here?"

"I came to find you."

He wanted to shake her for taking the chance, but he knew suddenly that it would always be this way, that she would never consider herself if danger threatened him. His arms tightened a little, unconsciously, about the small trembling body.

"But how, Marty? Why?"

"My father's dead. He died at the railroad camp. One of the paymasters brought the word. The news is all over town."

He tried to figure what the news might mean to them. Doc's death had freed them of their obligation to protect him. For a moment he was tempted to forget the dynamite, rush Marty through the tunnel and ride away, leaving the valley ranchers, the sheriff and the U.S. marshals to track down the stolen beef.

But the temptation did not last. He had started this. He would finish it.

"We've got to get out of here." He pushed Marty gently from him. "I have the dynamite." He indicated the box beside the tunnel entrance. "The cap is set. All we have to do is walk back to the other side, find a crevice to put the box in, unwrap the fuse and light it. The last beef has already gone through this tunnel, Marty."

"I wouldn't be too sure of that," Tim Younger's voice said.

Shamus almost reeled from the shock of it. Marty backed away stiffly until she stood in the tunnel entrance.

"Don't turn." Younger sounded almost amused. "You run into bad luck pretty often, Shamus. If I hadn't ridden in a few minutes ago and gone to kick Crowley out for some breakfast I wouldn't have known you were here."

Shamus did not say anything.

"Pull your gun and let it slide, Magee. You too, Marty, unless you want a bullet in his belly."

Shamus and Marty obeyed.

"All right," Younger said. "Now walk out of here, down the dump. No tricks. You first,

243

Shamus."

Magee turned slowly and started for the door. His head hung a little and his arms dangled at his sides as if he had given up the fight. He clumped on until he nearly reached the door. Then his left hand snaked out to grab Younger's gun. The gun exploded. He felt a hot tearing at his left side, but it did not stop him. He twisted the gun away and swung Younger around, holding him long enough to yell: "Through the tunnel, Marty — quick!"

She stared at him for a moment, wide eyed, and then to his horror she caught up the box of dynamite with its trailing fuse and ran into the tunnel mouth.

Younger cursed hoarsely, trying to wrench free of Shamus' grasp, trying to go after her. He almost got free, but Shamus tripped him.

They went down together, rolling across the rough floor, clawing at each other. Shamus tried to get a grip on Younger's throat and failed. They rolled into the drum of the old engine.

The bearded cable cut the back of Shamus' hand with its fuzz of broken wire, the pain stinging him as Younger twisted free and tried to crawl to the spot where Shamus had dropped his gun.

Shamus caught his leg with both hands and yanked him back, and Younger turned like a cornered animal. Snarling, he came up to his knees and sent a chopping blow at the side of Magee's neck. It missed, catching Magee on the shoulder, and Shamus grabbed the arm and flipped Younger onto his back.

Dimly he realized that Marty Clare had run back into the enginehouse and through the red haze in his brain he knew that she was shouting something.

He could not understand what she said, but as he managed to fasten his big hands around Younger's throat he had an instant to guess what she would be saying. She would be warn . . . And then it came, the shock wave from the explosion, driving air from the tunnel mouth with the force of a howitzer.

It sent Marty to her knees. It seemed to numb Younger, for he stopped struggling under Shamus' grasp. It filled the house with a deafening roar and tore loose boards from the outside wall.

Strangely Shamus was the least affected of the three. He released his grip on Younger's neck and scooped up his own gun from the floor.

He came up to his knees, and suddenly

found out how very weak he was. He had a roaring in his ears, too, an aftermath of the concussion from the blast.

"All right, Younger. Get up."

Younger rose slowly.

Shamus spoke to Marty without taking his eyes from the outlaw. "I wanted you to get through the tunnel, out of here. Now we're all blocked in together."

She said, "I'm sorry, Shamus. Honest I am. All I could think of was the tunnel, blocking it."

"You did that," he said dryly, "judging by the sound of the blast. It's lucky you weren't killed."

Younger began raging then. "You fools. You stupid goddam fools. What good do you think this will do you? Burton's men were closing in on the canyon mouth when I rode up this morning. The only reason they aren't up here now is because of the guards on the rims. You're trapped in here. I hope you're happy."

Shamus said, "You're trapped too, Tim. Think of that."

"I'll get out."

"Not while I'm pointing this gun at you, you won't. Was the sheriff with Burton?"

"What if he was?"

"I think it's about time we had a little law

in this. I think maybe you and I are going to walk down the canyon and do some talking."

"They'll hang you."

"Maybe. But if Luke Ronson is there I have my doubts. Luke shaped up as pretty much of a man at the saloon the other night, and when he hears Marty blew the tunnel to keep you from moving out the stolen meat he might be willing to listen to other things."

"Oh, what a fool." Younger shook his head in furious disbelief. "Don't you think that blast raised everyone in this town? Don't you think Ed Crowley's already spread the word that you're here, trying to spoil our game? You won't take me out of here, Shamus. A company of cavalry couldn't walk me the length of Main Street."

"He's right, Shamus," Marty said quietly. "You'll just get yourself killed."

"Maybe." Shamus set his jaw. "But I made mistakes, starting this, and I've got to get them straightened out."

Marty stared at him. "You *are* a fool — and I love you for it. Go ahead. I'm with you. Maybe they won't shoot at a woman."

He wished she would stay in the enginehouse, but he knew there was no good arguing with her. She came closer and saw the blood staining his coat.

"Shamus, you're hit!"

"Not too bad." Actually he did not know how serious the wound was, but it seemed to have stopped bleeding, and aside from a deep burning he felt no pain. "Get going, Younger. Down the dump, and be careful. Right now it would be a pleasure to shoot you in the back."

Younger gave him a long look and stepped out onto the slanting side of the dump. He had not exaggerated when he said that the blast had roused the town. The street below the hill was crowded with people.

Shamus spotted Ed Crowley in the front rank, and he called out to Crowley, while they were still a hundred feet above the level of the street.

"It's all over, Ed. The tunnel's blown."

Crowley began cursing him in a high, agonized voice and he cut the fat man short. "The rest of you better clear out."

An angry murmur swelled up. Shamus knew the sound. It was the sound of a mob, weak men, taking courage from their very numbers.

He said calmly, "You'd better listen to me. I've got Younger's gun and my own. That's ten shots, and Marty's got five more. Or were you planning to shoot down a woman?"

Younger shouted suddenly, "Take him and the girl. She blew the tunnel."

"That she did," Shamus said. "And you'd better listen. The game is over. Burton and the sheriff are at the lower end of the canyon. If you want to live you'll climb out of here with what you can carry right now. If you wait till Burton and the ranchers ride in they'll hang the lot of you. Move on, Younger."

He prodded the outlaw in the back with his gun. Younger slid on down the dump, and the crowd parted to let them pass.

Shamus was not sure the game was won, but he knew that any mob requires a leader and this one did not seem to have any. In fact men along the edges were already turning away, and by the time they came to the store more than half the crowd had faded into the old alleys, intent on climbing the steep mountain trails in their efforts to escape this canyon which had now become a death trap.

Crowley might have rallied them against Shamus, but Crowley was suffering from his own fears, not so much for bodily harm as for what Burton's men would do to his store and the rest of his beloved old town.

He stood on the steps, saying in a whining

voice, "You told me you'd put in a good word, Shamus. You promised."

Shamus looked at him and sighed. Younger was watching the melting crowd with bitter eyes. At last he said, "You've won, Shamus. Let me go."

"You burned the Burton ranch," Shamus said. "You set up this deal in stolen meat."

"The girl's father planned it. You can't keep him out."

"He's dead. I forgot you didn't know. I thought you overheard at the enginehouse."

He watched Younger's face break. Yes, Younger must have counted on this as his last card, the final play to save himself if everything else failed.

They were standing some ten feet apart, and Shamus had grown a little careless because Younger had no gun and the crowd was not backing him. He had let his arm swing down too far.

Younger moved with deadly speed. His right hand snaked under his coat. Out it came with a small gun, its twin barrels not over three inches long.

It had not occurred to Shamus that Younger would have a holdout stashed away somewhere. Such weapons were seldom carried by anyone save professional gamblers.

He reacted instinctively, but before he

could lift his heavy Colt the small bullet from the derringer struck his left shoulder.

Had it been a forty-five it would have knocked him down with its shocking power. As it was, his sixgun swung up evenly and he fired just as Younger emptied his second barrel. Younger's shot missed, but Shamus hit him squarely in the chest above the heart. Tim Younger died before his body reached the ground.

21

All movement on the street had ceased, and Ed Crowley's face above the black tangle of his beard was a yellow white. His fat hands trembled as he brought them up slowly in a kind of spreading gesture, to tell Shamus that he was not in this play.

Marty had given a little, wordless cry. Now she pressed forward to Shamus' side, taking his arm and trying to steer him to the porch.

"I'm all right." He dropped his Colt back into the holster, surprised to find that it was still in his hand. "I didn't know he had that little stingy gun, Marty."

The crowd came to life, but they did not move toward the store. Instead they turned away from it with increasing hurry. With the death of Younger, everything they had hoped for evaporated.

Marty forced Shamus into the store despite his protests. She led him into the kitchen and demanded hot water. She stripped off his coat and shirt.

The wound in his side was little more than a gouge, the bullet having plowed along the ribs without fracturing them. The hole in the shoulder was directly above the armpit, and the bullet had not come through.

Marty's face was so white that each freckle stood apart sharply. She said, "I've got to get it out of there."

"Huh?" he said, and winced. She was so very small, so very scared. "Better leave it alone, Marty."

"There isn't a doctor in a hundred miles. I think it struck a bone. I don't think it went too deep."

He said, "Those pepper boxes don't carry much of a powder charge, but let Crowley do it."

She curled her lip at the fat man. Crowley's hands were shaking so badly that he slopped the hot water as he tried to lift a pan from the stove. "I'll do it, Shamus. I've watched my father a hundred times. I wish I had a probe."

She got a cloth and sponged the wound,

cleaning the blood from the small, blue rimmed hole. "Get him a drink of whiskey, Crowley."

The fat man hurried to obey.

Shamus took the half filled water glass and drained it slowly. He was beginning to feel the letdown, but actually the hole in his shoulder did not hurt as much as he expected.

"Get a bullet out of your belt and bite down on the lead," she said. "And don't flinch."

He didn't flinch. When it was all over, when she had the little, misshapen piece of lead that had been a twenty-five caliber bullet, he was in better shape than she. She steadied herself, bandaging the shoulder, then his side.

Ed Crowley brought a new shirt and coat from his stock. She helped him into them, then rigged a sling for his left arm. Afterward she sat down. Her knees could no longer hold her.

Crowley offered whiskey. She refused, but took a cup of steaming coffee, nursing it, enjoying the warmth against her small palms.

"Probably some bone splinters," she said. "Probably that shoulder will be stiff. It's the best I could do."

And then she crumpled. Shamus caught her with his good arm. Shamus thought she was going to faint. She didn't. He said in a fussing voice, "You've got to rest, kid. Isn't there someplace, Ed, maybe up at the old mine, where she'll be safe, even when Burton's men ride in?"

"Where are you going?" Marty asked shakily.

"Down to meet them. Down to talk to the sheriff. I've got to try to save Ed's town."

"If you're that big a fool I'm going with you. They'll hang you if I don't."

He argued. As usual he got noplace. Crowley had to help him onto the horse. He couldn't imagine how awkward the lack of one hand made him.

They rode down the canyon, not hurrying. At the bend as they dropped out of the main street he looked back and saw Ed Crowley standing like a bearded mountain on the store porch, gazing after them.

He knew how Crowley felt. Everything he had, everything he had ever known, was tied up in the wreck of this town. Nothing would bring it back, but at least he could try to prevent the Bar X from burning the place. And the fault was his. If he had not ridden up here for a crew none of this need have happened.

Myra Dodge and Younger would have found a way if he had never come to Hawthorn, but he had been their goat. He could not escape the fact.

At the last canyon bend he motioned Marty to dismount and managed to lift himself clumsily from the saddle. They walked to the curve, peering carefully around the rock obstruction.

Burton's men were on the flat below them, dismounted, spread out beside the buildings of the old smelter. Between his position and theirs the canyon angled downward at a steep pitch, the cut so narrow that there was less than thirty feet between the footing of the rock walls.

He judged that Burton had attempted to ride into the canyon and the guards on the high rims above had turned the rancher back. He suspected that those guards were gone now, that word had been carried to them through the hills and that they had faded into the rough country under the ridge. But apparently the riders below did not know this.

They had built a fire in the lee of the smelter and seemed to be waiting for something.

Marty said, "I see the sheriff, over there, beyond the fire." Before Shamus guessed what she meant to do, she ran around the rock and came back on her horse.

"I'm going down to talk to them, Shamus. They won't shoot at a woman."

"Wait." He tried to catch her bridle with his free hand, but she pulled the animal sidewise and rode past. She turned the rock corner and the whang of a distant rifle cut through the stillness.

Shamus cursed, running forward as her horse went down, but she stepped out of the saddle and was on her feet when, he reached her. The rifle spat again, knocking loose rock over them as the bullet cut the wall above their heads.

He grabbed her arm, dragging her behind the shelter of the outthrust rock. He fairly shook with rage. This attack on Marty moved him as nothing else ever had in his whole life. He had never really believed the stories of Burton driving out the settler women and children. He had put them down to exaggerations by the rancher's enemies. Even Myra Dodge's story of being held captive had not aroused him as much as this. If he could reach Claude Burton now he would kill him joyfully.

"The damn murderers," he said.

"Maybe they didn't see who it was," Marty said. "Remember, the guards probably shot at them from the rim before we got here."

He forced himself to control his anger. He waited five minutes, then walked carefully around the rock. The men on the flat had mounted and bunched, and he could make out Burton's big form and Ronson's small one in front. "Sheriff! Sheriff! Can you hear me?" His voice roared down the slot of the canyon, echoing back and forth between the rock walls.

He listened. Ronson's voice replied, sounding weak and reedlike after his bellow: "I hear you."

"This is Shamus Magee. Younger and his men were butchering the stolen beef and carrying it through the old mine drainage tunnel to deliver to the railroad."

There was silence below, as if his statement had brought a kind of shock. Then Ronson's voice again: "Are they still doing it?"

"No. Younger's dead. I blew the tunnel. Most of them have cleared out."

"Thanks for telling us." It was Burton, and even in the distance he sounded sardonic. "We're coming in."

"No, wait. Marty Clare's in here with me. She had nothing to do with it. Let her ride out. Let her explain."

He saw Burton suddenly spur his horse

forward. The man seemed sure that he had nothing to fear from the canyon rims.

"She'll have to take her chances with the rest," Burton yelled. "Everybody in that canyon was mixed up in this."

Shamus heard the words and did not quite believe them. Not even Burton could be so pig-headed, so arbitrary. But Burton was riding ahead, and he had drawn his gun, and the men were beginning to follow him.

Shamus pulled his own gun. He said tensely across his shoulder, "Take my horse and pull back to Hawthorn. Get into the hills."

"No."

"Do as I say. If Burton comes around this corner I'm going to kill him."

But Burton never reached the corner. From the rim above them, there came a shout. Burton halted his horse and looked up. So did Shamus, and he saw Mushy Calder outlined on the jutting edge of a bare rock, his rifle thrust out before him.

"Burton!"

The rancher sat absolutely still on his horse. He had only his sixgun and he did not even try to lift it. The distance was far too great for a hand gun.

"I was headed out," the wolfer called, "and I got to thinking that I had to know what was going on back here. I'm going to kill you, Burton, the way you've killed other men. Without a chance. And I want you to know why you're dying. Remember that grey stallion?"

Burton swung his horse, bending over the animal's neck, driving home his spurs. Calder did not raise his rifle. He called, "It was a dumb thing to do, Burton. It started this whole mess. A lot of men have died because of it." And then he brought his gun up slowly.

It seemed to Shamus that Mushy Calder waited too long, that Burton was already out of effective range. But he forgot that Mushy was the best shot in the whole valley.

The report was surprisingly faint. Sound does not travel downward into a canyon as well as it does on the level. The rocks tend to reflect the waves.

Burton seemed to dive forward from his racing horse. He bounced once, and then he lay still in the trail. One or two of the men beyond him snapped shots at the small figure on the bare rocks. Calder ignored them.

"Sheriff." His voice was clear. "Ride up alone. You'll find out Shamus is telling the truth. The rest of you drop back to the smelter. The first man who tries to come into the canyon gets what Burton got."

For a minute or so a violent argument boiled among the mounted men. Then Ronson rode up alone, passing Burton's sprawled figure without even glancing at it, and came around the bend. He halted his horse, looking down on Shamus and the girl, his old face expressionless.

"You sure raised hell, boy."

Shamus started to answer, but thought better of it.

"Were you telling the truth?"

"Ride up and look at the tunnel," Shamus said. "Talk to Ed Crowley. And by the way. It wasn't Crowley's fault. Younger forced him into it. Don't let them burn his town."

Ronson said, "Nobody burns anything as long as I'm here."

Shamus wanted to remind him that he had not stopped Burton, but he held his peace. No one had ever stopped Burton as long as he lived.

"Can you get Marty out of here safely?" he asked Ronson.

"What about you?"

"There are paths up out of the canyon a man can use, if Mushy can hold them for an hour."

The sheriff's voice was dry. "Judging by

his performance I'd say he could hold them forever. Better take her with you. Some of the tempers are short down there. They'll get over it in time, but not today."

"What about charges?"

"I didn't see you shoot anyone." The sheriff sounded indifferent. "I'll run down Calder if I can, but I doubt he'll be caught. It would take half a day to climb to where he is, or nearly a day to ride around through the hills to the west. I suspect he'll be long gone from here by then."

He turned and rode back down the trail, a small figure, hunched forward on his horse as if he found the weight of his badge too much to carry right now.

Shamus looked upward. He could no longer see Calder.

"Mushy, you still there?"

Calder's head appeared around the edge of a rock.

"Can you hold them for a couple of hours while Marty and I ride back and climb out?"

"Hold them all day."

"Good luck, Mushy."

The wolfer did not answer. He was not a man to waste words.

Later that afternoon, as the sun slanted downward toward the west, Shamus and Marty followed the twisting ledge path to a break in the ridge and started down into the rough country to the north. Their horses were still in Pine Canyon, and they dropped down the northern slope with a speed that made a mockery of their slow ascent.

"We can cut over to the railroad camp," he told her.

"Let's don't. I'd rather ride east toward White Water. The Dodge woman is at the camp. I don't want to see her."

Shamus let her help him into the saddle. "Seems like she ought to be punished."

"She's punished," Marty said. "A woman like her wants things so badly that when she doesn't get them she hurts all over. What else could you do to her?"

Shamus shook his head. Looking at Marty's face he knew she had what she wanted. They were starting out with nothing. The future was unknown and uncertain. But to her it did not matter. She had confidence in him. The thought brought a funny feeling of contentment, a feeling he had never known before. By God, with Marty he could settle down and like it.

ABOUT THE AUTHOR

Todhunter Ballard began his career as an engineer, working on power plants and transmission lines. He turned to the world of letters via the editorship of an electrical trade magazine.

Since that time he has written more than 600 stories which have appeared in the world's leading magazines. He has also written numerous television shows, several screen plays and sixteen books. Among his most successful books are *Trail Town Marshal* and *Guns of the Lawless*.